D0098138

Whiteout!

Henry Mullins, a young cowboy from Southern California, sits back and watches the woman he loves marry someone else. That's when he decides to leave and ride off into the great unknown.

Intending to get to Los Angeles, he is forced inland by marauding Mexican bandits and eventually into the Sierra Nevadas, where he starts to trap wild animals to stay alive. Coming across a bi-annual meeting of trappers, he begins to learn the tricks of the trade and takes up trapping seriously.

Attacked by wolves, bears and the elements, Henry gradually learns the art of survival. And then he comes across a teepee with a beautiful squaw and her dying grandfather inside. Henry's life begins to change.

Winter sets in high in the mountains, Henry's first. And it turns out to be the biggest battle Henry has ever faced.

J M C P L
DISCARDED

*By the same author writing as
    Ben Ray*

Sharper
Sharper: Avenging Gun
Angel of Death: Sharper
Sharper's Revenge
Hell Riders
Sharper's Quest
Yellow Streak
Gunslingers
The Plains Killers
A Rolling Stone
Badge of Office
Black Smith
Mountain Trail
Hell on Horseback

Writing as Adam Smith
Money Thicker Than Blood
Death Came Calling
Stolen Fortunes

Writing as D.D. Lang
Woebegone
Last Stop Liberty
Death Storm
Burnout!
Deadly Venom
Blood Money

Writing as Will Black
Avenger from Hell
Tombstone Scarlet
The Legend of Broken
    Saddle
Death Comes Easy
Blood River

Writing as Del R. Doyle
Showdown at Ghost Creek
Blood at Ghost Creek
Rustlers at Ghost Creek
Ghost Creek Renegades

Whiteout!

Jay D. West

A Black Horse Western

ROBERT HALE

© Jay D. West 2018
First published in Great Britain 2018

ISBN 978-0-7198-2732-7

The Crowood Press
The Stable Block
Crowood Lane
Ramsbury
Marlborough
Wiltshire SN8 2HR

www.bhwesterns.com

Robert Hale is an imprint
of The Crowood Press

The right of Jay D. West to be identified as
author of this work has been asserted by him
in accordance with the Copyright, Designs and
Patents Act 1988

All rights reserved. No part of this publication may be
reproduced or transmitted in any form or by any means,
electronic or mechanical, including photocopying, recording,
or any information storage and retrieval system, without
permission in writing from the publishers.

Typeset by
Derek Doyle & Associates, Shaw Heath
Printed and bound in Great Britain by
4edge Limited

This one is for my beautiful grandchildren
Ellie, James, Reuben and Grace
with love

ONE

The last of the dying sunlight reflected off the bright red and yellow leaves of the scattered maples, sending beams of light like bright fingers into the dark woodland floor below. Henry Mullins stretched his lean frame and eased the aches and pains that filled his muscles and joints. The day had, as ever, been long and hard. Setting the traps in the morning and, hopefully, finding them all full come sundown, meant an evening of skinning and stretching and packing pelts ready for the bi-annual trip to the fur emporium near Walker Pass at the southern end of the Yosemite Valley. Henry sat staring at Half-Dome, a smooth, granite mountain that had been sliced in two by a glacier, the same glacier that had dug out Yosemite Valley and raised the mountains sky-ward creating waterfalls and altering the course of rivers. The sheer, rock wall of the strange-looking mountain never ceased to fascinate Henry. One day, he knew, he'd have to climb it just for the hell of it.

Winter was coming and there wasn't a thing Henry could do about that. Autumn usually lasted a week – ten days at the most, then the snows came, the rivers froze over and he'd be hunting white fur, getting that ready for the Spring trip.

The beaver had been plenty that summer, but the mountains were filling up with men. There was a time when Henry could go a whole year without seeing a single, living soul except at the Trading Post. Now, the mountains were crawling with men eager to trap the beaver for its valuable fur.

It had taken Henry nearly a whole year to discover why there were more and more trappers. It was all down to the sea otter, or rather, the lack of them. The otter had all but been extinct. Henry had heard tales of otters in rafts or schools of up to a hundred animals being killed in a matter of hours. They were killing them quicker than the otter could pup. The way things were going, the beaver would follow suit and then, maybe, the buffalo, too.

There was no way Henry could use all the meat left after skinning, and it grieved him to waste it. He kept what he needed, salting away meat for the winter in secret hidey-holes so that if worst came to worst, at least he'd have food when the snows came. The rest he left for the buzzards and mountain lions.

Henry was an entrepreneur, a free trapper. Not for him the restrictions of being what was commonly called engagers, men who were supplied and salaried by a major fur-trading company, neither was he a sharecropper, a man who operated on credit advanced by a company. No, Henry was a free man, but he had his doubts as to how long that would last.

Henry hadn't always been a trapper. In his youth, he'd been a farmer, a cattle roper and brander, fence builder, bronco buster – you name it, Henry had done it. Worked in a general store way down south near San Diego, but, there was never enough excitement for him.

He'd fallen in love and sat back, watching as she married someone else. That was when Henry decided to move on.

Leaving the rooming-house he'd spent six years at, six years in which he'd grown from youth to man, Mrs O'Reilly, the landlady, always treated him like a son and saw his departure as a betrayal – her little bird fleeing the nest.

Henry felt bad about it, but there was no way he could stay. At twenty-four years of age, Henry's possessions were packed up in two saddle-bags. Not much to show for a life, he'd mused.

Heading north from San Diego, he tried keeping to the coastline, his aim was Los Angeles and then maybe up to San Francisco or Sacramento. Mexican bandits forced him inland where the air was clammy and the temperature too hot for his liking, but he had little alternative.

Riding due east, it wasn't long before Henry had his first proper taste of the desert; the Mojave Desert. A great, yellow, barren area where it seemed impossible that anything could survive, let alone live there.

But he was wrong.

It didn't take Henry long to discover that the seemingly lifeless desert was teeming with wildlife.

Scorpions, rattlesnakes, sidewinders, lizards the like of which he never knew existed; wolves, coyotes and tracks of an even larger animal, that he shuddered to think what it was.

The days of riding had been torturous, the heat incessant, the light blinding as the sun reflected off the now almost bleached-white sand and bore into his eyes. Sweat stained his clothing, only to evaporate. Two of his five canteens had already been emptied and Henry hoped he'd find a place to rest up and refill his depleted water supply.

Naive though he was in the laws of Nature, Henry

knew that without water, he'd be dead quicker than crushing a bug under his boot.

His only constant companions were the buzzards that circled overhead. They circled and waited. Henry knew they were waiting on him.

That first night alone in the desert had been the scariest thing he'd ever done. The wailing of distant coyotes and some not so distant; the bark of what he thought were wolves or prairie-dogs, and the blood-curdling roar of pumas or mountain lions, set his nerves on edge.

Building a campfire had been easy enough, there was enough dried-out wood and kindling to last a lifetime.

Once the fire was lit, Henry's night-vision disappeared; all he could see was black, all he could hear were animal noises.

His first taste of snake – roasted over an open fire – had made him sick. The second mouthful made him gag, the third he managed to keep down and hardly noticed the rest.

The white meat kept his belly full and he took a liking to it. So much so, that it didn't take him long to try a lizard next, but the meat was tougher and had a strange taste, so Henry returned to snake-meat. The nights spent in the desert were freezing. After the heat of the day, the cold took on a sharper edge and no matter how close he got to the camp-fire, Henry awoke frequently, shivering, his teeth chattering so much his jawbone ached.

He survived. Henry reached the Sierra Nevada mountain range and that's when he began trapping.

First, just for food and clothing, but as the days turned into weeks and the weeks to months, Henry started to keep the pelts of the animals he managed to catch; jack-rabbits, an elk or two and even a puma, as he travelled northwards through the precipitous mountain range.

Making his own traps from whatever he could find, it was pretty much trial and error until, unexpectedly, he came across a rendezvous point where he met a whole bunch of trappers laden to the gills with fur. It made Henry's small load look insignificant when he saw the amount these veterans toted.

At first, the trappers were wary of a stranger in their camp. Solitary men by nature, the only time they congregated was at a rendezvous, usually set up by a fur-trading company, where a buyer would purchase everything they had.

Bales of beaver pelts were the favourite and Henry wondered how in the hell they caught so many. He had six.

He was soon recognized as a greenhorn, and that

made him safe in their company. Safe to the point where the grizzly trappers passed on some of their time-honoured skills.

Henry managed to raise thirty-seven dollars from his haul; some of the other men were coming away with the best part of a thousand dollars, more money than Henry had ever seen in his life.

It was here that Henry learned about the fur trade. About folks called Russians who operated further north, coming out of a place called Alaska, enslaving local Aleut and Kodiak Indians to do their trapping for them, as they lacked the skills. He heard of a strange country called China, somewhere over the Pacific Ocean. A country that bought all the fur it could get its hands on and traded back in silk and rare spices.

Most important of all, Henry bought his first beaver traps and a bottle of castoreum, a liquid that was obtained from beavers which gave off a musky odour that attracted the animal to its death. He also traded his town horse for a mule, reluctantly, but the mule would prove to be a better animal in the mountains.

Also traded in were Henry's town clothes. He bought a buckskin hunting shirt, leggings and moccasins. He learned that the fringes weren't just ornamental, they actually helped shed rain. The

13

buckskin was liberally greased to help with water-proofing and stank to high heaven and back. The Hawken rifle was a bargain. Henry was all for keeping his Sharps breech-loader, but soon saw the error of his ways.

The Hawken rifle had a shorter barrel and larger bore and the power of its heavy ball could kill a grizzly or a buffalo at up to two hundred yards. Being a percussion rifle, it was ignited by a copper cap – better in rain than a flintlock. Nothing worse, he was told, than being charged down by a grizzly, having it in your sights only for the rain to spoil the powder, and ending up the grizzly's supper.

Henry spent nearly a week at the rendezvous before, one by one and without saying a word, the trappers drifted back to their isolation, getting ready for the winter and to start trapping for the next rendezvous.

There were no written laws of the mountain man's existence, only the unwritten ones: you don't steal traps from another trapper, and you don't hunt in their neck of the woods.

There was enough killing and robbery going on as it was. A whole year's supply of pelts could be lost in one unguarded moment.

So, loaded up with a half-dozen traps, a wooden bottle full of castoreum, some ground pemmican, jerky, a hunting knife, a bag of nuts, the Hawken rifle and ammunition, a Colt Frontiersman with a box of slugs, empty sacks and a mule, Henry set off to hunt in earnest.

Travelling north, he followed streams and rivers for two or three days. Catching his first deer, he had enough fresh meat to last him for a week, and enough to salt down and stash away.

The winding river that threaded its way through the mountains, drained out into a long, wide valley and Henry saw the beaver dam and smiled. Now it was time to find out if he remembered all he'd been told.

Grabbing the sack that contained his traps, Henry walked upstream for half a mile so that the beavers wouldn't be able to smell him. Using a wooden stake to anchor the heavy, baited traps underwater in what he hoped to be a beaver runway, he smeared castoreum on the stake as he'd been told, and got out of the water, his feet and legs freezing.

All he had to do now was wait.

Henry waited and fell asleep; only the insistent braying of the mule woke him up.

Henry drew his pistol but for the life of him saw nothing to shoot at. He dozed some more and the mule quietened down and continued to graze on the rich grasslands that ran alongside the riverbank.

Gazing towards the sun, Henry tried to estimate how long he'd been asleep. He hadn't got a clue. He'd forgotten to sight the sun before he slept!

Walking upstream again, Henry decided to check on the first trap. Success. His first trapped beaver, dead, having drowned in the water, awaited him.

Releasing the trap, Henry lifted the animal out of the water, a fine specimen weighing in, he estimated, at fifty or sixty pounds, then tossed it to the riverbank, then re-set the trap. Now to practise skinning.

Cutting the tail off to use later for food, Henry slit the animal open along the belly from head to tail-less end, allowing the guts to spill out freely. The guts sent up a shower of steam and a foul smell that Henry could well have done without.

The skin came off the body like butter off a knife and Henry cut off the legs just above the paws and pulled the stumps through, freeing the pelt.

Fishing through the guts, he found what he hoped to be the castoreum gland and placed it carefully in the deer-hide pouch attached to his belt. All he had to do now was find something he could use as a graining block and clean the pelt's underside.

Lifting the pelt, Henry was amazed at how heavy it felt in comparison to the ones he'd caught by shooting them with his Sharps a couple of weeks earlier.

This is going to be easy, he thought to himself. He was never to utter that sentence again.

TWO

Trapping beaver did become easier. The heavy, metal traps were the only danger, apart from being attacked by angry beavers of course.

Setting the traps, coating the fix-stick with castoreum and then waiting became an everyday event and pretty soon, Henry was building up quite a collection of beaver pelts, tails and castoreum glands. Trouble was, he was getting a bit tired of eating tails and beaver meat. He tried every which way of cooking them, boiling, frying, stewing, but the taste was always the same: strong and tough.

Loneliness was also playing a part in his existence. Although that's what Henry sought, the reality – only having the mule to talk to – was not an exciting prospect.

As the summer began to die and the quick spread

of autumn permeated the mountains and valleys below, the air became crisper. Henry had spent most of the summer in the valleys by the side of the swift-running river that the beavers continually dammed up, and he'd made only occasional forays up high; he'd seen mountain goats and had tried to catch one for its milk but failed miserably.

He'd killed another deer and the change in his diet was welcome. Skinning the deer proved harder than the beaver, but he needed the skin to repair his moccasins and he'd also need a shelter for the winter.

For four months now, Henry had slept each night under the stars; rain had been the biggest problem, the heavy squalls often waking him in the middle of the night and soaking him to the skin. He seemed to be continually wet or damp or both and Henry noticed that some of his joints were getting stiffer each morning, so a shelter for the winter became a priority.

The skin on his face had gone a deep brown, calluses and blisters covered his hands but they were becoming easier now as the skin toughened, and Henry took to bathing in the fast-flowing waters, using his knife to shave, and then running around like a madman and rolling in the grass to dry off; if anyone had seen him in that state, buck-naked with a white body but deeply-tanned face and hands, they'd've skedaddled back to civilization, vowing never more to enter the mountains!

Fishing was the next thing Henry tried. The river was full of salmon, at least that's what Henry thought they were. They were certainly big and although he'd never eaten fish in his life, it couldn't be any worse than deer or beaver and the occasional handful of nuts and berries that had so far supplemented his diet.

Cutting a sapling, Henry made a spear by whittling down one end and, standing thigh-deep in the cold water, he waited for a fish to swim by.

He didn't have long to wait. Time and again he thrust the makeshift spear into the water, but each time he missed. Getting the angle right was the biggest problem, the water seemed to distort how far away the fish were, they to be within touching distance of the spear, but Henry just kept right on missing.

The spear broke as the point, missing a fish by inches, rammed into the rocky river-bed. Undaunted, Henry made another, and another after that. Then he caught his first fish.

Whooping with delight, he flicked the fish on to the riverbank where it struggled to both extricate itself from the spear and get back into the water.

Using his knife-handle Henry stunned the fish, and pulled the spear free. Within minutes, he had a fire going and fashioned a spit from twigs and hung the fish over the flames.

It was only later that he realized he should've taken out the guts first. The salmon's stomach swelled and, as it cooked, burst open where the spear had punctured it and almost doused the fire.

The smell of the cooking meat was so different to anything Henry had experienced before and as the scales began to burn off, his mouth watered as he watched the light-pink flesh slowly darken.

Finally, he could wait no longer. Burning his fingertips, he held the fish as he stuck his Bowie knife in and sliced off a hunk of fish. It was moist and full of oil and tasted better than anything he'd ever had in his life.

Lying back beside the fire, Henry rested. The meat had been filling, more so than beaver or deer, and he felt his eyes begin to close. He tried to resist the temptation to take a nap, but thought, what the hell! I'm a free man. I can do whatever, whenever I want. Henry closed his eyes and slept.

Was it a dream?

The gentle roaring seemed to fill Henry's head and he kept his eyes closed and didn't move.

21

There was a strange smell, dank, that seemed to waft over him. He heard the heavy footfalls and even heavier breathing, coupled with snorts and grunts.

Slowly, Henry opened one eye. The sun, still high in the sky and as bright as ever, made his one-eyed vision come out all blue and unfocused. He was conscious of his eye-lashes. He seemed to be able to see each one as clear as clear.

But nothing else.

Whatever animal was by his campsite was out of his field of vision and Henry was loath to turn his head for fear of attracting the beast.

Then he heard a higher-pitched whimper and lighter footfalls that moved quicker and, quick as a flash, a large, hairy head loomed over Henry's face from behind.

A long, pink tongue darted out and licked his nose and it was all Henry could do not to scream out. He closed his eye and waited to see what would happen next. His whole body began to shake from the inside out and mentally he said a prayer.

Another long lick from the rough, pink tongue. This time down his cheek. Henry was like a rock statue he'd seen once in the centre square in San Diego: unmoveable.

A loud growl to his left and the smaller creature

bounded away. Henry felt, rather than saw it as the sun's rays hit his face once more.

Cautiously, he opened an eye again.

What he saw filled him with dread. On the other side of the now-dying campfire sat a grizzly and two cubs. The cubs were playfully fighting each other, rolling round in the dirt without a care in the world. The giant grizzly sat sniffing the air and keeping a watchful eye on the terrain.

In one giant paw sat the remains of Henry's meal and the grizzly held it out so the cubs could attack it, which they did with gusto.

Henry knew then it was a female. It was the first real-live bear Henry had ever had the misfortune to come across. He only hoped it would be his last!

Slowly, the giant bear stood on its hind legs. Henry's eye moved up with it and fear gripped his belly. Jesus! he thought, that dang thing is almost twelve-feet tall! He swallowed, hard. The movement of his Adam's apple didn't go unnoticed by the bear.

A deep growl of warning rent the air and the cubs froze. Henry couldn't freeze any more than he already had.

Trying his damnedest not to blink, Henry watched as the giant animal began lumbering towards him.

23

He had two choices: run like hell, although he didn't think he could out-run a full-grown bear; or play possum. He opted for the latter.

A chill seemed to fill him; the sun's rays were cut off as the huge animal loomed over him. Hardly daring to breathe, Henry waited on the outcome.

A paw, almost twice the thickness of Henry's neck, gently nudged him. There was no animosity there, the bear wasn't trying to maul him, just see if he was alive or dead.

Another poke, this time a little harder, but not painful. Then as Henry closed his eye, the bear got down on to all fours and Henry tasted rather than smelled, the fetid breath of the animal. He heard the sniffs as she took in his body scent, felt her tongue gingerly touch his face and lick. Salt, Henry had time to think.

A growl, that seemed no more than six inches from his face, almost made Henry jump out of his skin, and it was all he could do not to panic.

A snort, sounding dismissive, followed and Henry heard the heavy footfalls receding. A lighter growl and the cubs, who hadn't moved a muscle, gave their rendition of a growl, high-pitched, like cats mewing.

Henry opened his eye again and watched as the three bears ambled down to the riverbank.

The cubs sat on their haunches and waited while their mother slowly walked into the river and stood on a submerged rock and she too, waited.

Turning his head, feeling slightly easier now but nowhere near out of danger, Henry watched the motionless mother-bear. With reflexes quicker than an animal that size had a right to, a giant paw splashed down into the turbulent waters and a huge fish arced through the air, landing almost atop the cubs.

Then another, and another followed.

Satisfied, the bear left the river and joined the cubs, and her teeth made short work of the struggling fish. The cubs, on the other hand, seemed to be playing with their meal. Jumping up on all fours, patting the flailing fish on the side, picking it up in their teeth and tossing it into the air before they, too, began to eat.

The cubs took no notice of their surroundings once they had the fish, but Henry noticed that the mother-bear rarely looked down. She sat on her haunches, holding the now-dead fish in her paws and kept sentinel over her family, pausing every now and then as a sound or a scent reached her.

Ten minutes later, the three bears ambled slowly and confidently back into the woods.

Henry realized suddenly what the bears were

doing. From somewhere in the distant past he recalled his old schoolmarm explaining hibernation and she'd used bears as an example. How the animals built up their body fat to last them through their winter sleep.

It made sense to Henry. He had a lean frame, one that he felt sure would feel the cold. Right there and then, Henry decided to follow the example of the bears. He, too, would build up his body fat, that way, he reasoned, he'd stand a better chance of surviving the winter.

Then, feeling as if he'd held his breath for an hour or more, breathed in so deep he thought his chest would burst, and the same time that he pissed his pants, sweat broke out all over his body and the shakes came.

Yet still he didn't dare move. So sure was he that the mother-bear was keeping a weather-eye on him that he decided to stay put for another ten minutes or so – just to make sure.

Lying on your back next to a dying campfire knowing there were critters out there that could snap your spine as easy as a twig, made the time drag for Henry, but he was strong in his will and, if anything, the bears had taught him two very useful lessons: never relax your guard for a moment and eat well for winter!

He smiled to himself and shifted his butt, the piss had soaked through now and the warmth had turned cold. Maybe he'd take a dip in the river. Then he decided not to shave any more either. Maybe a beard would keep his face warm.

From that day on, Henry was very careful where and when he took a nap.

THREE

The beaver disappeared.

Henry had set his traps as usual in the beaver-runs and had then set off into the forest to gather nuts and berries to make some more pemmican.

Apart from sequoias or giant redwoods, which were easy to name, Henry really didn't have any idea of the plant life in this area of California. He ate berries by trial and error and he'd made a few errors. Sickness and vomiting gave him reason not to try a certain kind of berry again, and it also told him to maybe try two or three instead of a handful.

How he wished he'd paid more attention at school when the schoolmarm had talked of plants and trees and animals. Try as he might, he could recall little of what she'd said.

Henry gathered up hazelnuts that grew wild and

28

stashed them in his 'possible sack'. He had no idea why it was called that, but that's what the other trappers had called it. It was simply a sack that contained tobacco, pemmican, ammunition and whatever else you felt like putting in it. One thing they told him was never lose sight of your possible sack, and Henry never did.

He saw signs of wild life, deer droppings, a freshly-trampled weed or broken sapling, but caught no sight of anything to aim at.

He wasn't overly bothered. He still had salted venison stashed away and if all else failed, there was always a beaver tail or two.

The day was drawing on and Henry decided to have a pipe before heading back to the river. Propping himself up on a tree-stump, he went through the ritual of airing and filling his pipe, making sure the tobacco wasn't packed too tight, else it wouldn't light, nor too loose in which case it'd burn down too quick and that would be a waste.

As it was, he didn't think he'd have enough tobacco to last him until the next rendezvous, assuming he was able to find the place again.

Striking one of the matches kept in a tin box in his possible sack, Henry puffed on the pipe, not inhaling yet, just intent on getting it started. A great cloud of blue-white smoke hung over him in the dank, still air of the forest. The pipe glowed red and Henry doused the match, carefully making sure it was out before tossing it to the ground. Folding his arms across his chest, he sucked in deeply through the pipe and inhaled the smoke, feeling a little dizzy as it filled his lungs, enjoyed every moment of it.

The silence of the forest was both reassuring and a little daunting. The countryside and mountains were always full of some noise or other, birds singing, the rush of the water and, higher up, the song of the wind as it blew between rocks.

Gazing up into the almost-bare canopy of the forest, Henry realized, not for the first time, that winter would be only a matter of weeks away now. The forest floor was littered with leaves and small branches and the smell of rotting vegetation that rose was stronger than ever.

Idly puffing on his pipe, Henry was suddenly tense.

From behind him he heard the soft crackle as if a twig was being broken in half.

Since the visit of the grizzly and two cubs, Henry had been just a tad wary of unexpected and unexplained noises.

He grabbed the Frontiersman from his belt, he found the holster cumbersome, so just hooked the pistol it through his belt instead. Cocking the hammer as quietly as he could, he pulled himself up on his knees, held his breath and listened.

The silence was deafening.

Then another soft crackle, and another. Still he couldn't see anything. Maybe it was a rabbit, or a deer, he hoped, feeding off the forest floor. But the ominous silence, no bird singing or calls, told him otherwise. Whatever had made those noises was a predator, not a forager.

Casting an eye around his situation, Henry tried to find a tree he could clamber up and give himself the benefit of some height, but the trees' barks were smooth and had no lower branches for him to climb up; he was stuck on the ground with an unseen enemy lurking nearby.

Despite the dank atmosphere, beads of sweat formed on Henry's forehead. He'd long ago ceased to be frightened as such, but he was awful wary of wild critters making a meal out of him. He wasn't ready to die just yet.

Then he saw the eyes.

No more than ten feet from where he knelt, almost perfectly camouflaged, were a pair of evil-looking, yellow eyes that stared, unblinking into his.

It was, Henry felt sure, a wolf!

Swallowing deeply and hard, Henry might not know much yet about the wild, but one thing he did know was that wolves roamed and hunted in packs. They were not solitary creatures.

Trying to keep a fix on the pair of eyes, Henry quickly scanned around him to see if there were any more. He couldn't see any, but what the hell did that matter? If they were there, he'd find out soon enough.

The eyes staring at him didn't waver and in the noiseless atmosphere, Henry could now just pick up the faint sound of panting as the wolf, doubtless its long, pink tongue lolling to one side of its razor-toothed mouth, breathed in and out.

There was a crunch that almost made Henry jump. Without realizing it, he'd bitten through the stem of his pipe, so tightly was he gripping it between clenched teeth.

Relax, he told himself. Relax and think. What would the wolf try? Would he try anything? Sure he would, if he was hungry, he told himself.

Maybe he was just not hungry. Maybe the wolf had never seen a man before, at least, a white man.

Henry waited. His short time out in the wilds had taught him how to do that. Wait. Wait and see.

A sudden rustle from above made Henry point the pistol skywards. A bird, unable to stand the tension no doubt, flew out from a branch into a clearing in the canopy. It must have been two- to three-hundred feet above Henry's head and as the weak, late-summer sunlight reflected off its wings, it seemed to glow with a golden hue.

The huge bird's head craned downwards as if staring at Henry and asking: What the hell are you doing in my back yard?

Henry could almost see the bird's eyes, which seemed red-tinted, as it flew majestically out of sight.

Returning his gaze to find the yellow eyes once more, Henry panicked.

They'd gone.

Frantically, he scoured the area to his left and right and straight ahead, but he could see nothing. Whatever it was had moved on. Maybe the bird, an eagle, Henry thought, had scared the wolf off? He doubted it. What Henry really thought was that the wolf was on a recce and pretty soon he'd return with the pack and try to get themselves a meal.

Henry wasn't about to hang around and find out.

Keeping his Colt handy, he stuck the broken stem of his pipe back in his mouth; it still glowed and he couldn't see the point in discarding it and wasting his precious baccy, and he raised himself to his feet in a crouching position.

Hanging his possible sack over his shoulder, he retrieved the Hawken rifle from the tree-stump and held it tightly in his left hand. The Colt, shaking slightly now, was in his right.

He backtracked to the deer run he'd been following, alert, keeping his eyes skinned for the slightest movement; Henry all but tip-toed out of the forest.

As he reached the edge, he scoured the grassland in front of him that led down to the riverbank. He heard bird calls, the rush of water over submerged rocks, and the scampering of small critters through the tall grass.

What he didn't want to see was the tall grass bending unnaturally. He knew if he saw that, then the wolf was out there waiting for him to make a move.

As he watched, the grasses swayed gently in the breeze back and fro, that was all, they just swayed the way God had intended.

Slowly, Henry emerged from the forest and made his way towards his temporary campsite. He'd build the fire up. Critters didn't like fire much, he remembered, and he'd be safer there.

The small clearing, ten feet from the riverbank, was a mess. Henry had tethered his mule on a long rein so that the animal could graze, but something had been rummaging through the pelt bale and sticking their snout into things that didn't concern them.

Two or three half-eaten beaver tails lay in the dirt, but as far as Henry could tell, that was all.

Placing the Hawken against a rock, and keeping the Colt levelled, Henry began building up the almost extinguished campfire. The dried grass caught straight away, and he added larger pieces of wood until the flames crackled three and four feet high.

The heat reached his face and Henry realized just how cold it had been in the forest. Walking round the campsite to make sure it was clear, Henry decided to check out the traps. There were six of them, all empty.

But each trap was snapped closed!

Henry froze.

Someone or something was nearby. He could sense it.

Keeping his Colt as level as his shaking hand could manage, his eyes darted every which way, looking for the slightest movement, his ears listening for the sound.

He neither heard nor saw anything.

His reasoning told him that if it were another grizzly, he'd have heard it by now. There was no way a critter that big could either hide successfully or keep quiet enough, so whatever it was, it wasn't a bear. That thought cheered him some.

On the other hand, it could be a mountain lion. They could sure hide well enough and spring on you from out of nowhere.

The low growl was almost inaudible, but it seemed to drift in on the slow, cooling breeze. Henry instinctively knew it was a wolf. The very same wolf that had been spying on him in the forest.

Keeping low with his pistol at the ready, Henry made his way back towards the campfire. If the wolf – or wolves – was getting ready to jump him, he wanted the fire nearby.

Thrusting a dried-out, two-foot-long log into the flames, Henry watched as it caught fire. It would, he knew, be a useful weapon as those critters sure didn't like flames.

The growl drifted in once more. The mule whinnied. Henry had forgotten all about the damn mule!

Keeping the burning log in front of him and the Colt ready, Henry backed off towards the mule. The beast wasn't tethered, but it wouldn't move. Obviously, he'd caught the scent of something, and whatever it was, he didn't like it none too much.

Grabbing the rein with his Colt hand, Henry tried to drag the animal nearer the campfire. Stubbornly, the mule dug its hoofs in and remained exactly where it was.

'Goddamnit!' Henry muttered quietly. 'You wanna git yourself killed?' He tugged hard on the rope rein, but the mule had made its mind up. Here is where it stood and here is where it would stay.

Using the torch as a prod, Henry held it behind the mule's rear end. That moved it, all right. Henry then had trouble stopping the damn thing. His right arm was almost pulled out if its socket as the mule surged forward. The flames from the torch had more of an effect than the threat of a wolf.

Calming the animal down, Henry allowed the rein to drop to the ground once more and the stubborn mule began grazing again as if nothing was wrong.

Sweat was breaking out on Henry's forehead now as the effort of pulling the mule closer, and the tension of an imminent attack by an unseen enemy, began to take its toll. Licking his lips, Henry crouched down and waited.

He heard the low growl for a third time, but still could neither see nor place which direction it was coming in from.

A sudden thought hit Henry right between the eyesand he silently cursed himself for being so dumb.

If it was a wolf, how the hell did it release the

beaver traps?

The realization that there could be more than one 'thing' stalking Henry, made him even more wary.

Apart from the rushing flow of the river over the rock-bed, silence reigned supreme. For ten minutes now, there had been no more growls.

Then a rock, seemingly from nowhere, arced from across the campsite and thudded into a small crop of bushes. The wolf, which had been hiding, let out a yelp of pain as the stone struck home.

With a speed quicker than Henry would have thought possible, the wolf leapt into view and raced straight at him. The log was almost out and the animal's speed took him by surprise. Henry caught the beast on the shoulder with the log and the smell of burning hair filled his nostrils. He tried to cock the Colt, but the wolf was too quick for him.

Sinking its teeth into his left arm and twisting its head, Henry felt the skin break as the fangs pierced his flesh.

The attack, however, was defensive. All the wolf was interested in was getting to safety as fast as possible and no sooner had its fangs punctured Henry's arm, than it sped off, back towards the forest and anonymity.

For a moment or two, Henry was frozen. The

rock, the wolf's attack and escape, had been so fast that they'd barely had time to register in Henry's brain.

Then he felt the warm stickiness between the fingers of his left hand and saw the red of his own blood.

'Jesus!' Henry shouted out and the echo reverberated off the low mountains on the other side of the river, coming back to him as if to mock.

Pulling off his doeskin jacket, Henry rolled up the sodden sleeve of his long-and inspected the wound.

A neat, almost semi-circle of holes, each leaking blood, greeted his eyes.

'Goddamnit it to hell!' he muttered.

One thing Henry did know was that a bite could get infected. Rabies was a constant threat with any wild creature, that and dirt and insects.

Henry walked to the river and thrust his arm into the freezing-cold water. He didn't notice the temperature though, as he watched the eddying waters dilute the blood. Slim fingers of blood hung in the water for seconds before being whisked away and turned invisible.

The cold water did the trick. Pretty soon, the bleeding stopped, and Henry knew what he had to do next to maybe help him survive in case the animal was rabid.

Drying his arm on the doeskin of his trousers, Henry walked back to the campfire and grabbed his possible sack.

Inside was an elkhorn powder container with a brass screw-top. He removed the stopper and took a deep breath.

He still had some matches left but needed to conserve them, so thrust a small twig into the campfire.

Pouring the powder on to the open wounds, Henry leaned forward, picked up a chunk of wood and gripped it tightly in his teeth – real tight.

He took the now-burning twig and, taking a final deep breath as sweat ran down his face and back in a torrent, he ignited the black powder that covered his left forearm.

The small thud of a dull explosion masked the grunt he let out from between his clenched teeth. The smell of burning flesh filled his nostrils as Henry fell over backwards, out like a light.

Clouds scudded across a dark sky, masking the full moon. For a few moments, Henry was aware of nothing but those clouds racing overhead. Black in the centre but with a blue-white tinge to the outsides where the moon's rays hit.

Looking to his left, Henry saw the dying embers

of the campfire glow red and then grey as the breeze hit and then receded.

Then he felt the pain.

Never a drinking man, Henry nevertheless had a bottle of whiskey wrapped in doeskin for protection, hidden in his possible sack.

Not only did he feel the need now to take a swig, he knew he'd better sterilize the burns – and fast.

Unwrapping the bottle, he pulled the cork out with his teeth and gulped down three mouthfuls of the sharp liquid. It burned its way down his throat and hit his stomach like a sledgehammer and he couldn't stop the coughing.

Eyes watering, the sweat on his head and most other parts of his body feeling cold, Henry poured whiskey on his arm.

The pain of the burn from the black-powder had been bad enough, but he'd not had to suffer that for too long as unconsciousness had taken over. The hot bite of the whiskey, now over a much larger wound, was like nothing he'd ever experienced before.

Henry Mullins screamed like a banshee.

In his torment, he heard the distant howls of coyotes or wolves, seeming to answer his own yell of pain.

Staring at the mess that was once his forearm,

Henry looked at the blister that had formed: nearly six inches long and three wide, tapering at each end. His arm felt as though the whiskey were burning its way through flesh, muscle, sinew and then melting his bones.

And all the while the constant throb of pain filled his head.

Henry still couldn't rest up. He needed to bandage that arm and maybe make himself a sling, keep it as still as possible until the scabs formed – or until he knew he hadn't got rabies.

Using the only spare clothing he had, a fresh pair of long-johns that hadn't been worn yet, he cut the top into strips, leaving the leggings alone as he could always wear them.

Then, from some dark recess of his brain, he remembered moss. He had no idea how he'd recalled someone once, many years ago, being burned badly when a hayloft caught fire and a bale had landed on the man's back.

The doc then, what was his name? Henry couldn't remember, had covered the burned skin with damp moss before bandaging.

Pulling himself to his feet, surprised he could even stand, let alone walk, Henry made his way across the open ground towards the now dark and foreboding forest.

There were enough scattered rocks on the perimeter of the tree-line to scrape off all the moss he'd need. He carried it back to the campsite and sat again, his head reeling with pain.

Gently, he placed the cool, moist moss on his burned forearm, wincing as he did it. But the pain did begin to recede. Whatever properties the moss had, it sure began to work fast.

Picking up a strip of makeshift bandage, Henry held one end in his teeth and, with his right hand, began winding around and around as tight as he could bear it.

He wrapped four bandages altogether, cutting and tying each one as he went.

The arm still throbbed. Henry's whole body seemed to throb, but the pain was dull now, an inconvenience, something he'd have to put up with.

Then he began to shiver.

Maybe shock, he thought, as his body started trembling uncontrollably. He threw some wood on to the almost extinguished campfire and some tinder he had left, on top of that. Stupid, he mouthed, he should've done that the other way around. But the campfire caught hold and pretty soon, bright yellow and red flames danced in the air, sending a plume of sparks up in its thermal.

The brightness of the night disappeared as his

eyes became used to the light of the fire, making everything else seem black for a while.

Henry took another two slugs of the whiskey then re-corked it. He never knew when he might need to use it again, and getting drunk now was not a good idea. Welcome, sure, but not a good idea.

With his arm and the campfire taken care of, Henry fashioned a sling out of a bright-yellow Shoshone scarf that he'd obtained at the last rendezvous. Carefully, he slid his arm inside it and again, the pain seemed to lessen.

Maybe he could sleep now, he thought.

The baying in the distance took up once more as, for reasons best known to themselves, the wolves howled away at the moon.

The clouds passed and the moon, bright and round and seeming to be within touching distance, grinned down on Henry.

With a pain-furrowed brow, Henry closed his eyes and tried to sleep.

FOUR

Henry Mullins spent the night in considerable pain, his sleep only coming in fits and starts, and he was wide awake as the sun crested the mountain tops.

The pain in his arm had eased to a dull throb and he found it difficult to make a fist.

Chilled by the early morning air, Henry raised himself to his knees and stacked up the campfire once more, making a mental note to gather some more wood soon, else he'd run out.

His head began to swim, and Henry thought he was going to black out, but the symptoms didn't last long. Blood rushing to his head, he thought.

The fire soon caught again, and as the flames rose high, Henry felt the heat on his face and hands.

Standing now, he made his way down to the river-bank and sank the tin pot in the water, filling it to overflowing. He tipped this over his head, shivering as the icy-cold water ran down his face and neck. He filled the pot again and brought it back to the fire, where he hung it over the flames to heat. His head ached, his eyes were sore, and every joint cried out to him as he waited for the water to boil.

He'd been warned about rheumatism, the trapper's biggest enemy. Being almost continually damp without drying off was no good for a body and, although Henry hadn't been trapping for long, he knew what these first faint twinges heralded.

Steam began to rise from the flame-blackened pot and Henry threw in a handful of beans; no day could begin without coffee. Today, though, there would be no breakfast; Henry had no appetite at all.

He sat pondering the beaver traps. How the hell had they all closed? Surely not by a wolf? 'No, impossible,' he said out loud – too loud as he heard the echo come back.

Henry wrapped a bandanna around the pot-handle and poured the thick, black brew into his tin mug which he balanced between his legs. Working with only one good arm was going to be difficult, he decided.

He'd heard no noises during the night; either he'd slept longer than he thought, or he had blacked out and been unconscious to. But if the wolf had been around, it would have attacked him while he slept; the smell of blood must have been strong in the animal's snout.

The plain fact of the matter was, the wolf hadn't attacked.

Therefore, Henry deduced, it wasn't around any more.

Sipping his coffee, he felt the warmth sink to his stomach and began to feel more human.

The sun finally cleared the mountain tops and the first full rays of the day crept over the campsite and that made him feel better too.

Henry had no doubt that he'd have to move on. If there were pelt-stealers following him, it would only be a matter of time before they found his stash, took the lot and maybe killed him into the bargain.

Reckoning he was at the north end of the Sierra Nevadas, the river would be the Humboldt, flowing east to west. Henry had seen a map at the last rendezvous and had memorized as much as he could, planning on getting one himself, only to discover they were scarcer than gold-dust.

Closing his eyes, he tried to picture the map: Sierra Nevadas, Humboldt River. To the east, following the river, he'd hit the north-end of the Rockies, ending up in Salt Lake City, but that would mean passing through Crow and Sioux country, something he didn't want to do. To the west, the river flowed to the Pacific Ocean, crossing Northern Paiute and Modoc Indian land.

Henry reckoned he was stuck between a rock and a hard place. North, he thought. A whole mess of smaller tribes leading into Canada before hitting Blackfoot Country.

There was no point in thinking south. He'd come from that direction.

Still with closed eyes, Henry tried to recall the site for the next rendezvous. He knew it was at the northern end of the Yosemite Valley; he also knew it was near a trading post and horse-station that the army ran, but couldn't remember the name.

No matter, he thought, it'd come back to him.

Rooting through his possible sack, Henry found his ledger. Each day, he marked how many pelts he had and the possible worth. To date, Henry had over two hundred beaver pelts and sixty-three deer skins all baled up, weighing in at around fifty-pounds each. He'd reckoned nine hundred to a thousand dollars – at least.

It was a fortune to him, but he still had to get it to the rendezvous, and he only had one good arm!

As he sat sipping his coffee, he suddenly caught sight of the merest wisp of smoke.

Was he seeing things?

Henry put the mug down and stared straight ahead, his vision ready to pick up on anything that moved.

He caught another brief glimpse as the smoke dissipated in the air. Henry sniffed, thrusting his head forward, as if that helped. But he was upwind, whatever smell there might be didn't reach him.

He checked his Colt. It was still loaded with five slugs, so he added another to the empty chamber and stood. Having a rough idea where the smoke was coming from, Henry lumbered forward; lumbered being the operative word, he thought, as his legs felt decidedly unsteady.

It could be nothing. It could be a natural fire caused by the sun, or it could be a campsite. If it were the latter, they were going to a lot of trouble in concealing their whereabouts.

The going wasn't easy. From the sandy riverbank, the trail led through scrub and rock, before skirting the forest and going up at least a hundred feet.

Animals had obviously used the route as, here and there, bare patches of soil showed between clumps of grass and bramble, so Henry figured on there being a pathway; mountain track, more than likely he reasoned.

Reaching the crest of the rise, Henry slowed down some. Maintaining his balance, keeping the Colt level and not being able to use his left arm had plain worn him out and he needed a breather. The sun, although not as hot as it would be later that day, still gave off enough heat to make him sweat, along with his exertions.

Breathing heavily, Henry rested, the throbbing in his arm worse now than it had been all night as the blood coursed through his veins. He could feel the beat of his heart thudding in his chest. That wolf sure had a lot to answer for, he thought ruefully.

Stretching his back and flexing the muscles in his legs, Henry then crouched down, trying to peer over the crest at whatever hid behind it.

What he saw fairly took his breath away.

Nestled in a small, grassy patch beneath a curve of trees was a teepee. There was a campfire to one side of it, along with a drying frame and a blanket stretched out on the ground.

On the wooden frame were pieces of jerky drying in the sun and a couple of beaver pelts strung up to dry, with the fleshy side facing the sun's rays.

Over the campfire on a wooden tripod, hung a metal basin. Henry could see that there was no smoke coming up from the fire. He'd heard how

Indian's had a knack of either making plenty of smoke or none at all.

The camp looked deserted, although he knew that could not be the case. A small, grey pony was tethered on the other side of the teepee – it had no saddle.

As Henry watched, a figure came out of the teepee. She was beautiful. Her long, black hair flowed freely, and she wore a dress of doeskin, brightly-painted and adorned with beads. She wore moccasin boots that again were brightly-painted. Henry thought, even at this distance, she was the most beautiful woman he'd ever seen.

What to do now? He didn't want to frighten her, and he didn't want to leave. He had to meet her.

As he watched, she knelt on the blanket beside the fire, and began pounding something in a rock-bowl. He couldn't see what it was, but she worked at it steadily.

Henry holstered his side-iron and stood on legs that almost gave way under him.

Still, she didn't look up, so intent was she on her chores.

Henry began to descend the steep path towards the teepee, taking small, silent steps so as not to alarm the woman. He was only half-way down when she suddenly stopped what she was doing and looked up – straight at Henry.

Standing, she ran inside the teepee only to reappear, almost instantly, armed with a spear.

FIVE

Henry's forward momentum carried him down the slope another six or seven paces before he managed to come to a halt. The woman, girl really, was in a crouched position, the spear gripped firmly in both hands – not for throwing, but for jabbing.

Henry raised his right hand in the time-honoured Indian gesture of peace, but the girl steadfastly refused to acknowledge him. As far as she was concerned, he was the enemy and she would kill him – if she had to.

'I come in peace,' Henry said as he stared into the biggest and darkest brown eyes he'd ever seen.

The girl didn't answer. As far as Henry knew, she may not even understand what he was saying.

'I mean you no harm,' Henry tried again.

The girl jabbed at him menacingly with the spear even though they were separated by at least twenty feet.

Henry kept his arm raised as a gesture of good will, but his legs were shaking. He didn't know if it was nerves or the result of the attack by the wolf.

The stand-off continued for a few silent minutes before Henry lowered his arm. The girl saw that movement as the first sign of an attack and she growled, jabbing with the spear. Then she brought the spear up as if to throw it.

There was nothing Henry could do. He could draw his side-iron, he knew that, but he didn't want to show any antagonism towards her. He could turn and walk away, but she could still throw that spear and kill him. How could she let him walk away without fearing that he'd sneak back later, after dark maybe, and kill her?

As it turned out, Henry didn't have to do anything. Whether it was the wolf attack, the heat, the fear of death looming or whatever, Henry's legs buckled beneath him and, try as he might, he couldn't stop himself from collapsing to the hard, rocky ground.

He remained there, in a heap, unconscious.

*

Henry's eyes fluttered open. Then closed.

He opened them again almost involuntarily. He was lying on his back in a soft place. He was used to sleeping rough by now, the hardness of the ground had long since ceased to keep him awake.

But the softness he now lay on had brought him out of unconsciousness. He stared straight up, wondering what in the hell it was he was looking at.

There was a bright circle of light, through which faint wisps of smoke passed. The circle was also marred by black rods, joined at the top with what looked like horsehair rope.

Then he felt the cool cloth on his forehead. He brought his right hand up to his head and felt the cloth – doeskin, soaked in water and just plain resting on his head.

Henry went to sit up, but the pain in his head and left arm told him otherwise.

He tried to think, tried to recall what had happened, but failed. He couldn't remember a damn thing!

Resting again, trying to get his bearings, Henry concentrated on the only reality he could see. The bright circle of light.

As he stared, he saw white, puffy clouds scud past, their whiteness intensified by the blue of the sky.

High above, almost in and out of the clouds, a black speck seemed to float in a descending spiral. A bird. A large bird, maybe a buzzard, Henry thought.

A cough from his left brought him back to earth. The cough came again and the hair on the back of Henry's neck bristled.

In pain, Henry turned his head in the direction of the noise.

It was dark. The bright light from above shone down on Henry's face, making the interior seem even blacker than it really was. It took a few moments for his eyes to get used to the darkness, but, gradually, shapes began to appear.

Then he saw the old man. An old Indian man.

Instinctively, Henry's right hand moved to his holster. He needed to feel the reassuring coldness of the Colt.

It wasn't there, neither was his gun-belt.

Panic didn't set in, but it wasn't far off coming, as Henry stared at the wizened, lined brown face of the sleeping man.

Asleep, the man coughed again. It was a dry, rattling cough, that permeated everywhere. It was the cough of a dying man. A death-rattle of a cough.

A triangle of light broke through and, centred in the triangle, a black shape moved inside, keeping one arm on the flap that allowed the light to enter.

The girl!

Everything came back to Henry in a flood, a painful recall of memory.

The figure framed in the triangle of light remained motionless. She wasn't looking at Henry, her head was turned towards the old man. She was watching and listening. Seeming satisfied that all was well, her head turned towards Henry.

She stared at him for full minutes without uttering a sound or making a move, then she let the flap close the triangle of light and walked across the rock-floor to Henry.

Squatting by his side silently, she felt the doeskin on his forehead, took it off, immersed it in a buffalo-hide bucket that Henry hadn't seen, wrung it out and, before replacing it, laid her palm on his forehead.

The touch sent a wave of feeling through Henry's body that he'd never felt before in his life.

He felt no pain. He felt as light as a feather. He felt immortal.

The Indian girl removed her hand, obviously satisfied that Henry was alive and that his temperature had dropped or at least, hadn't got any worse.

She replaced the doeskin and stood, turned away from him and walked back towards the entrance.

'Thank you,' Henry said.

The girl turned and, although Henry couldn't see her face, he felt sure she smiled at him. He hoped she smiled, anyway.

He closed his eyes once again and, without either realizing it or wanting it particularly, he drifted back into a combination of sleep and unconsciousness.

The circle of light was gone.

It was pitch black and eerily silent.

Then he heard the breathing. Low, shallow, almost a pant with a rasp every now and then, like a boot scraping across shale.

Henry tried to sit bolt upright, but his legs were tied together, and he felt the pull of rope on his neck.

The effort of trying to sit up had tugged on the rope round his neck and this had dislodged a stick, which in turn had knocked a metal plate; these had fallen on to another metal plate.

The noise seemed to fill the small enclosure. Teepee! Suddenly, Henry knew where he was and how he'd got there. Then he remembered the girl.

A bright orange-yellow light entered. He couldn't see behind it or either side of it; but the holder could see him.

Henry began to cough.

The torch was lowered slightly, and Henry could

see the whites of eyes and the flash of teeth but nothing else.

He realized that it wasn't a rope round his neck; it was a strip of leather, probably buffalo, and he'd tightened it as he'd tried to sit up. The leather was tight round his neck – too tight – and Henry was beginning to have trouble breathing.

He saw the flash of a blade as it reflected off the torch and Henry thought his time had come. He closed his eyes and waited for death.

Instead, he felt the pull of the leather as the knife sawed its way through and he gulped in air as the pressure lessened. The throbbing that had begun to build up behind his eyeballs diminished; he was still trussed, but felt free.

'Thanks,' he managed to cough out. There was no reply. The torch moved across to the other side of the teepee and Henry got a better look at the old-timer who was still asleep.

The Indian girl lowered the torch until, it seemed to Henry, she was about to set the old man's long, grey hair alight.

The girl squatted by the silent body and stared intently at the sleeping man's face.

From where he was, Henry could see the almost serene expression on the old Indian's features; he couldn't see any movement though. The silence in the teepee was broken by a high-pitched wailing that sent a shiver down Henry's spine and set his arm to throbbing with a vengeance.

SIX

The girl sat by the side of the dead man all night. Henry reckoned it must have been her father or grandfather, perhaps.

She'd stopped wailing after about an hour but then set in to a constant chanting. Henry couldn't make out a single word she was saying as she sat, cross-legged on the ground, rocking backwards and forwards and repeating over and over the same chant.

Eventually, Henry drifted off into a half sleep, the constant drone of her voice waking him every so often.

As the sun rose, so the chanting stopped in the teepee. From outside, Henry could hear chopping and managed to loosen his ropes and get up to leave the teepee for the first time.

The squaw was busy weaving saplings and branches together and took no notice of Henry at all. He asked if there was anything he could do.

The girl seemed to understand what he'd said, for she merely looked down at his left arm and then back up to his eyes as if to say, 'with one arm you can't help.' So Henry sat and watched her work.

After about an hour, a platform began to emerge from the saplings and branches that stood five feet from the ground. The girl worked silently and quickly, seeming to know exactly what she was doing.

Using a horsehair rope, she began pulling at the platform and it rose majestically into the air, but she couldn't hold it.

Henry jumped up and grabbed hold of the rope just as it seemed to be slipping out of the girl's grasp.

For the first time, she smiled at him and the darker complexion of her face seemed to make her perfectly-formed teeth shine like a beacon.

A wave swept over Henry as she smiled, but the smile was short-lived. As soon as the platform was aloft, resting on four legs, she tied the rope round a rock and then began lashing more rope at the top of each leg, making sure the platform was secure.

Satisfied, she entered the teepee, closing the flap

behind her.

Whatever she was about to do in there, Henry thought, it was obvious she didn't want him watching.

From inside the teepee, Henry heard the chanting once more, so he made himself comfort-able and waited. Henry was good at waiting.

He helped himself to some water and watched as the sun rose higher in the sky. Henry reckoned an hour had passed before the teepee flap opened and the girl emerged.

She was dressed in another doeskin dress, but this one was pure white. She wore feathers in her hair and her body was adorned with beads. Henry couldn't help marvelling at how beautiful she was.

Alongside the platform were two poles joined together at one end to form a V-shape. The space in between was covered with buffalo hide to form a sort of stretcher. The girl pulled the poles inside the teepee, leaving the flap open. Henry stood and followed her inside.

What he saw made his jaw fall wide open.

The old man on the cot opposite Henry's, had been completely re-dressed. He wore a war bonnet of eagle feathers, the tail of which ran down almost the entire length of his body. A doeskin jacket and breeches, ornately embroidered with beads had replaced the white linen shift he'd been wearing. His arms were crossed over his chest and, in his left hand was an eagle feather, in his right, an arrow.

Around his waist were various pouches that seemed to be full of grass, but on closer inspection, Henry realized it was jerky in some and pemmican in others. Food for the after-world no doubt, Henry mused.

The squaw looked up at Henry, and the look told him exactly what she wanted. He moved to the feet of the dead man as she moved to his head and gently placed her hands under the dead man's shoulders and lifted. Henry had little time to think about how strong but frail the girl looked.

Henry hooked his good arm beneath both legs and guided them on to the frame that had been placed beside the cot. She lashed the body firmly to the frame and then they grabbed a pole each and dragged the body outside.

The squaw pointed to where the frame should be laid down and between them, they wrestled the body to the foot of the platform, the V-end closest.

Tying a rope to the pointed end of the frame, she looped the other end over the top of the platform then began pulling. Little by little, the platform began to lift into the air and she motioned Henry to take over from her while she moved the two poles forward until the frame was vertical, resting on one end of the platform.

Amazing Henry again with her strength, the squaw began lifting the frame as Henry pulled the rope and slowly, the frame was eased into position atop the platform.

Sweat was pouring from Henry's body at the exertion of lugging the body aloft, but as he looked at the girl, she was as dry as a bone, not a sign of sweat.

Without acknowledging Henry's help, she began to gather brush and tinder and branches together which she placed beneath the platform. Realization hit Henry like a hammer. It was a funeral pyre. Why it hadn't occurred to him before, he couldn't say, maybe he was sicker than he thought.

Backing off, he rested by the side of the teepee and watched as she piled the tinder high, then grabbing a burning branch from the campfire, she thrust it into the pile.

The flames began licking their way higher and higher, but she placed the fire in such a position that the legs of the platform would remain standing until the end. The base of the platform caught, and the air was filled with the sickly-sweet smell of burning flesh. Henry wasn't too sure whether it was the old man or the doeskin he was wearing, but he shifted from his down-wind position as he began to gag. The last thing he wanted was to be sick and lose face in front of the Indian girl.

Meanwhile, the squaw was down on her knees, the chant coming from her lips was different somehow. Henry had never been a church-going man, but sometimes, if he'd been passing the church on a Sunday, he'd hear the congregation singing a hymn or two and there was one particular hymn that seemed similar to the chant the squaw was singing in a low-pitched voice.

Suddenly, she raised her arms above her head as the thick white smoke rose into the heavens and a shiver ran down Henry's back.

He didn't know much about Indian customs and suchlike, but the meaning seemed obvious, even to him. It was as if the girl was celebrating the release of the dead man's soul or spirit; it seemed to be wafting up in the smoke.

Again, the smile appeared on the squaw's face. The chanting reached a high pitch and then abruptly stopped.

All the hairs on Henry's neck were standing to attention: both at the sound of the chant and now, at the ensuing silence.

Slowly and gracefully, the squaw stood, her head still bowed, eyes closed. She lifted her head, opened her eyes and crossed her arms over her chest. She stood like that for ten minutes as Henry watched, fascinated.

With a crack and a crash, the platform collapsed into itself sending a shower of flame and sparks high into the sky.

This seemed to be what the girl had been waiting for, it was like another sign, another release from the human body.

Bowing her head again, but only momentarily, she left the side of the pyre without once looking back.

She approached Henry, and to his amazement, bowed down in front of him as if in supplication.

Henry gazed down at her thick, black hair; studied her bare, brown arms and felt a wave of pure joy sweep over him.

The girl raised her head and, gesturing with her hands, she pointed at herself and then at Henry and then she cradled her fingers together, locking them as one.

It took a while for Henry to comprehend what she was trying to convey. And when he did, he just couldn't believe it!

The girl was telling him that she was his.

'No, no,' he started, 'you don't have to do that!'

The girl looked into Henry's eyes, and he looked down into hers and melted instantly.

Taking her offered hand, he helped her to her feet.

As she stood in front of him, Henry went to release her hand, but she gripped his hard and gradually began to lead him back inside the teepee.

Henry followed, unable to take his eyes off her. Not wanting to, either.

SEVEN

They lay together for three hours, fully clothed and in silence. Henry didn't know what to make of her or what she wanted.

Initially, he'd tried talking to her, but it was obvious she couldn't speak the white man's tongue, so he contented himself with just holding her.

The squaw slept for most of the time, hardly surprising, Henry thought, as she'd been up all night.

When she awoke, she sat bolt upright and stared at Henry as if for the first time. He smiled. She returned it, but it was a false smile as she recalled the previous night and the funeral pyre of that very morning.

Standing, she left the teepee and Henry followed.

Outside, the sun shone brightly, though there was a slight tinge of coldness in the breeze; the onset of winter, Henry mused. The squaw stared at the embers of the pyre. Every now and then a spark of flame would flare and then die down again as the breeze disturbed the ashes.

Of the old man, there was not a visible sign, but the ashes in the centre of the pyre showed a disfigured outline of where he was. It would take many more hours for the body to be completely consumed by the hot ashes.

The squaw began piling up branches and twigs on the pyre once more and pretty soon there was a blazing inferno; even now, that sweet, burning-flesh smell was still all too apparent.

To take his mind off what was happening, Henry took stock of the campsite. It was his first contact with Indians and he marvelled at the sophistication and ingenuity.

The teepee, which Henry noted was as solid as any shack he'd ever seen, but a damn sight better insulated, was a masterpiece of construction. Surrounding a conical frame of poles, slightly tilted to give more headroom, buffalo hide was stretched and sewn together with sinews, lodge pins secured the covering, except for the entrance hole, which had a triangular-shaped door flap. The top of the teepee was open and the poles, tied together with rawhide, were exposed.

The opening formed a chimney and the buffalo flap was held open by a separate pole, which could be moved according to the wind changes, that way the teepee was mostly smoke-free inside.

To one side of the teepee was a wood frame where snowshoes hung and there was also a buffalo bladder bag with a doeskin top containing fresh water. On top of the frame were strips of jerky drying in the sun, and a freshly-smoked and greased deerskin.

The tools and utensils seemed very basic to Henry; a flesher with an elkhorn handle and metal blade, a horn spoon and scraper made of buffalo bone with a leather grip, a small rawhide box decorated with brightly-painted symbols, and a bowl that seemed to be made of solid rock.

There seemed to be plenty of buffalo meat about. Over the small, smokeless campfire hung a metal pot and Henry could smell sage, and when he looked closer, saw prairie turnips and wild peas and onions that fair set his mouth to watering.

Spread on a rawhide blanket were freshly-made pemmican cakes, buffalo meat and ground and dried berries. Henry helped himself to one. They were a damn sight better than the ones he'd bought at the last rendezvous.

The squaw had crept up behind him and, as

Henry turned, he almost jumped out of his skin, spitting pemmican cake down his jacket. The girl laughed at this, and Henry felt himself redden with embarrassment.

To ease his situation, Henry pointed at his chest and said, 'Henry. Me, Henry.' Then he pointed at her.

She copied him exactly, pointing to herself and mouthing the name, but it came out as, 'Hearney, me Hearney.'

'No, no,' Henry started again, slapping his chest with the palm of his hand. 'Me Henry!'

The girl seemed to understand this time and pointed at Henry's chest, mouthing, 'Hearney.'

'Henry.'

'Hearney.'

'Hen-ry.'

'Hear-ney.'

'Hell, that's close enough,' Henry said at last. Then he pointed at her chest.

The squaw looked down at his pointing finger and then at her own chest. The sound that escaped her lips as she pointed to herself was totally incomprehensible to Henry. All but the last part which sounded like Mint. So that's what he called her, Mint.

'You Mint, me Henry,' Henry said and smiled.

'Me Mint, you Hear-ney,' she replied.

'That'll do,' he said.

'Hear-ney,' Mint said and put her hands to her mouth.

'Eat?' Henry guessed.

'Eat,' Mint replied, pointing to the pot over the campfire.

'Ready to eat a horse,' Henry said.

Mint just gave him a puzzled look, a frown creasing her brow.

'Doesn't matter,' Henry said, guiding her towards the fire, 'it doesn't matter.'

They sat and ate the buffalo stew and Henry couldn't remember the last time he'd enjoyed a meal so much. The meat was tender, and the vegetables tasted like nothing on earth.

'Good,' Henry said, 'very good.'

'Good?' Mint asked.

Henry rubbed his stomach and smiled.

Mint did the same and smiled, flashing her brilliant, white teeth.

She busied herself for the next hour tidying away. It was obvious to Henry that she was going wherever he went. He watched as she expertly packed away everything into rawhide sacks and boxes. The poles from the teepee were used as a travois, which she hitched up behind her pony. In next to no time, the campsite was bare, the fire out and it would have taken a tracker all his time to suss out who'd been there.

Except for the still-smouldering funeral pyre.

Mint stood in what seemed like silent prayer for a few moments before she slipped atop her saddle-less pony, motioning for Henry to ride the other horse, the one that had belonged to the old man.

Henry stared long and hard at the white pony with a large, black spot that crossed over one eye. The pony did likewise, eyeing Henry.

There was no bridle or bit, no reins, nothing. Mint held on to her pony by gripping the mane and using her knees. Henry had one good arm and he'd never ridden without a saddle, except maybe when he was a kid.

Seeing his plight, Mint dismounted and led his pony to a pile of rocks on the edge of the old camp-site. Henry clambered up the rocks and merely stepped on to the pony as Mint held it. The pony didn't bat an eyelid.

Making sure his wounded arm was comfortable in his sling, Henry gripped the animal's mane as tightly as he dared; he sure didn't want to hurt the pony because that could result in him being thrown.

Mint mounted up once more and he watched the

graceful lines of her body, and sighed. Henry guessed she was sixteen or seventeen at the most.

Digging her moccasins into the pony's flanks, Mint started up the rocky pathway that only yesterday Henry had descended, and he followed in her wake.

The mule was exactly where Henry had left it the previous day; it didn't even look up as the two riders approached. Mint helped Henry pack his own stuff up and they loaded it all on to the mule who seemed resigned to his fate. The mule all the while eyed the two ponies with suspicion.

Henry saw no reason to change his planned route of following the Humboldt River east. He'd heard about the great Salt Lake that he'd have to cross, but he wanted to get to the Rockies before winter set in.

Already, the red leaves were beginning to turn brown and Henry could feel the faint edge to the breeze on his face. Casting his eyes skywards, the deep blue of the summer sky seemed a little paler somehow, and there was a yellowish tinge to the horizon.

When winter came, it would come like an avalanche and they needed to prepare a winter site.

Henry dismounted and retrieved his beaver traps. On an impulse, Henry held one of the closed traps out, showing it to Mint. The lowering of her eyes told him all he needed to know. It was she who had set them off and it would take Henry another six months to find out why.

EIGHT

Their progress was slow as they first ascended rocky slopes and then descended into lush green valleys before they hit the plains and were able to follow the river with relative ease.

With the beaver having finished moulting, he still had time to trap some for their pelts, their tails for food and build up his supply of castoreum glands before the waters started freezing over.

Within a week, the first snow flurries hit them. Small flakes, hardly making any difference to the landscape. The tops of the now distant mountains were obscured by the low-lying clouds, but every now and then there'd be a break and Henry could see their white caps quite clearly. It was his first sighting of snow.

He'd talked the hind leg off a mule to Mint, trying

to teach her at least the basics so that they could talk. She, in turn, had tried teaching him her own language, but with little success; while she thrived on the new experience, Henry had floundered.

Although they'd shared the same cot, they still hadn't slept together. Mint had been loving and caring and he'd taught her how to kiss the white man's way after she'd shown him that rubbing noses could be a shared experience.

Henry wanted the girl. It was as simple as that.

He'd fallen in love with her at first sight and she'd done nothing to change his mind. For the first time since leaving southern California all those months ago, Henry didn't give his childhood sweetheart another thought.

The breeze had turned into a sharp wind and Mint gave Henry a buffalo hide jacket that had been dyed red. The coat fit him like a glove and he felt warmer.

The only problem he had was the fact that his arm was taking a damn sight longer to heal that he would have thought. The skin was not closing over the wounds. Scabs would form, but with the slightest movement, they'd break open again, or seep a putrid ooze that stank to high hell.

Pretty soon, Henry discovered that Mint could teach him more than he could ever teach her. She

knew which plants to eat, where to find the wild vegetables, peas, turnips some carrots and even winter
cabbage. She could make deer, beaver tail or
buffalo taste like steak and even her jerky was the
best he'd ever had, moist and chewy.

Pemmican cake was her speciality and Henry
never tired of it, even though the berries stained his
lips a vivid red for days on end.

She soothed the sores on his injured arm, wrapping herbs into the bandages to help the healing,
but despite all her efforts, the wounds were slow to
mend.

The snow had now started in earnest. The balmy
Indian summer that they'd experienced for a
couple of days, vanished overnight. A stiff north-
easterly blew up, bending the tops of the pines as
they trudged eastwards.

The wind was so strong and the fall of snow so
heavy, that conversation – even attempted conversation – proved impossible.

This left Henry with a lot of time during the day
to think. One thing was puzzling him. Although he
wasn't an expert on Indian traditions by any stretch
of the imagination, he couldn't ever recall hearing
about funeral pyres.

He'd heard that dead warriors, whether killed in
battle or from natural causes, were left to rot on the

death platform, so that their spirits could rise to wherever Indian spirits rose to.

Mint rode in silence, her heavy buffalo-skin cloak was growing whiter by the minute, and with her head bowed against the wind, he could see very little of her.

As he turned to make sure she was OK, a sudden thought of the old Indian Sasquatch came to mind.

Although the white men called it Big Foot, it was the same thing; a wild, giant mountain-man that no one could either prove or disprove.

Mint, covered as she was in buffalo hide, riding atop her pinto and covered in snow, looked exactly like Henry could picture the wild man.

He grinned to himself. Maybe that's how these legends started, he thought.

Reining in, Henry thought the weather was getting too bad to travel any further. Visibility was practically nil, he could hardly see the ground in front of him.

He motioned to Mint that they should make camp and shelter while they still could. She couldn't see him, and Henry had to grab the mane of her pony to halt her.

The biting cold and the driving wind had taken its toll on their strength.

When Henry had been at his first rendezvous,

he'd heard tales of men freezing to death in their saddles as they rode; then of their mounts freezing to death, making a macabre frozen statue until the thaws came.

One of the old-timers had four fingers missing from his left hand, a hand he'd used to lead his mule. It wasn't, he said, until he came to let go of the reins that he realized his fingers were frozen solid and as he'd tried to free the reins with his right hand, the fingers had snapped off and he hadn't felt a thing. Not until later that night, he'd said, when he'd managed to get a fire going.

Henry hadn't known whether to believe him or not, but it was better to be safe than sorry.

Henry hadn't gotten any gloves, it was difficult enough to set the traps as it was and gloves were an extra hindrance; if you needed to shoot quickly before your target disappeared, gloves were impossible. Mounted, they were a necessity. Henry had fashioned a beaver pelt, with the fur inwards, so that his hands were covered from the chill winds and he'd kept flexing his fingers – just to make sure he could still feel them.

His feet, however, were a different story. Try as he might to exercise his toes, the feeling was beginning to leave and the feeling of a damp coldness was creeping up his shins.

81

Mint wore thick, dear-hide boots, also with the fur inside. Wrapped around her shoulders was a huge piece of buffalo hide and, although some of her legs were bare, she seemed to show no outward sign of discomfort.

Dismounting, Henry indicated, as best he could to Mint, that they should set up camp for the night. Mint shook her head and pointed ahead. Henry looked but could see nothing but a white wall of snow falling from the heavens. Then he figured Mint must know the terrain and that she knew a better place to camp.

Waving her forward, Henry followed, leading the mule on foot in an effort to get some feeling back in his feet.

Mint led in silence for nearly half an hour before she slipped soundlessly from her pony and led the way between two large rocks that formed a V.

Henry marvelled not only that she knew they were there, but also, how the hell she'd found them.

The wind seemed to blow less as they passed between the rocks, the snow came in short flurries as if eager not to fill up the basin Henry found himself in.

Visibility was better, too, and in the rock wall that faced him, he saw the small, dark opening. A cave.

Without waiting, Mint led her pony to the opening and within a few minutes, had a campfire burning brightly. Henry didn't see any matches; the dry tinder that littered the cave floor seemed to catch fire by magic.

Henry staked out the pony and his mule close to the cave entrance and, getting down on hands and knees, he crawled inside.

The silence that greeted him only went to tell him how noisy the wind had been outside. He hadn't noticed then, he guessed he just got used to the continual howling so that he paid it no heed. But, as the heat from the fire seeped through his skin, his ears began to ring, and he realized just how cold he had felt.

A tingling sensation began in his hands and pretty soon, a real deep hurt set in as sensation came back to his fingertips. Holding his hands in front of the fire, he saw how white and blue his fingers were, right down to the second joint.

Mint pushed his hands further away from the flames, afraid, Henry thought, that he'd burn himself. Then she began to remove first her own boots, and then Henry's moccasins.

If Henry thought the stinging in his fingers was bad, it was nothing compared to the agony he suffered with his feet. It was all he could do to stop himself from screaming as, bit by bit, feeling and blood began to flow back into his extremities.

Mint didn't seem to suffer at all, if she did, Henry couldn't see any sign of pain in her young face. She looked just as serene and beautiful as ever. Henry, however, clenched his teeth really tight. There was no way he was going to lose face in front of Mint.

After thirty minutes, the pain subsided, and Henry was able to think about eating and drinking. Now that he felt warmer, his stomach told him how hungry he was.

As if Mint had read his mind, she began preparing a stew. Using the fresh snow for boiling-water, she chopped up carrots and turnip and added sage and something Henry wasn't too familiar with, and threw them in the pot that she'd hung over the fire. They still had deer meat left and, after the vegetables had been boiling away for a few minutes, Mint added the meat.

Henry got his old pot out of his possible sack, filled it with snow and waited for it to boil – he figured Indians didn't drink coffee, although he was none too sure about that.

The small cave was soon filled with the enticing aromas of the stew and the fresh boiling coffee and these smells seemed to take all the hardship of the day away. For the first time since sunup, Henry felt relaxed, cosy, and ready for anything.

What he hadn't figured on was Mint.

She began by unpacking buffalo hide from the travois, which she carefully laid out at the back of the cave, forming a bed. Adding fuel to the fire, she began melting more snow in two large pots, which she then allowed to stand for a while to cool down.

Henry lit his pipe as he watched her move silently around the cave. Using two short teepee poles and more hide, she fashioned a cover for the cave entrance, and then placed one of the pots outside for the ponies and mule to drink. Closing the cover, the cave became almost windproof.

Taking the other pot, Mint moved to the rear of the cave and set the now cooling water down on the stone floor and, before Henry could stop her, she slipped out of her doe-skin dress and stood naked before him, a small inviting smile filled her lips.

Slowly and carefully, she began washing her body and Henry couldn't take his eyes off her.

Her skin was as smooth as a peach, the colour of a spring-time fawn and there wasn't a blemish to be seen.

Her small breasts, with water dripping off them, were a delight to behold. Drying herself off just as slowly and carefully as she'd washed herself, Mint clambered between the buffalo-hides and left one side open, looking at Henry.

It didn't take Henry long to understand the implication.

Dousing his pipe, he stood too quickly, banging his head on the roof of the cave, that made him see stars. Undaunted, he all but tore off his coat and shirt, but had a deal of trouble untying the leather belt; it was still damp. Dropping his trousers to the ground, Henry, still clad in what used to be white long-johns, joined Mint in the makeshift bed.

She giggled gloriously at his modesty and slowly, very slowly, began to undo the buttons on Henry's long-johns.

NINE

That night Henry didn't get much sleep, but when they did eventually drift off into a comfortable doze, the sun – unseen because of the raging blizzard – was just beginning to rise.

Although the wind had died a little, the snow was still falling heavily and, as Henry opened the flap of their makeshift door, all he could see was a wall of white.

He closed the flap and turned to look at the sleeping face of Mint: she had the face of an angel, he thought, as he stared at her flawless complexion.

Her eyes opened and instantly she smiled up at his face. Lifting her right hand, she stroked his cheek; there was no need for words.

Even with one arm, their lovemaking had been the best thing Henry had ever experienced and the thoughts of the previous night ran around his head like a loose cannonball as he leant forward and kissed Mint gently on her lips. The response was instant as she threw her arms around his neck and all but dragged him on top of her, forcing the air from his lungs. Henry had never felt so happy.

They held each other for a few moments before Henry broke free of her embrace. Love or not, he thought, he sure was hungry, and his mouth sang out for coffee.

Getting to his knees Henry pulled on his long-johns, forced his legs through the soft, doeskin trousers which were still damp from the snow, pulled his shirt on and arranged his left arm back in its sling.

There was no headroom in the small cave, it was impossible to stand, so Henry crawled around on his knees, getting the kindling they'd saved from the previous night so that they could light a fire.

Mint sprang up, her bare breasts seeming like diamonds to Henry and a wave of emotion swept over him: if they were to die out here in the middle of nowhere, he thanked God he was with Mint.

She dressed quickly. She'd seen what Henry was about to try do and, in her culture, that was her role.

Brushing him aside, Mint soon had a small fire going, large enough to melt snow in the coffee pot and boil water for Henry's coffee. While that was happening, she folded up the blankets and the buffalo covering from their bed and tidied them away, creating more space in the cramped tent.

Mint dug out some root vegetables that had already been boiled and placed them in Henry's tin pan and held it over the flames. She added small pieces of raw deer meat, some nuts and berries and fried them all together.

The smell was driving Henry wild, whether because of his physical exertions of the night before or not, he had never been so hungry in his life.

As the coffee boiled, Mint spooned out the mixture from the pan on to two plates and handed one to Henry. It was hot, too hot to use his fingers as Mint did, so he used the bone spoon that was still in the pot, to eat. Mint giggled as she watched him consume his food.

Henry poured himself some coffee and then held the pot towards Mint, indicating that he wondered if she drank the stuff.

She looked at it quizzically for a few moments, then nodded. Henry smiled as he poured her a small mugful then waited while she sniffed it, before taking the mug slowly towards her lips.

As she'd seen Henry do, she blew on the surface on the hot coffee to cool it slightly before taking a first tentative sip.

Her expression changed at once to one of utter distaste as she spat out the coffee on the ground beside her, she stuck her tongue out and wiped it with the back of her sleeve, trying to get rid of the taste and all the time going, 'ugh!'

Henry couldn't help himself, he just plain laughed his head off. He remembered, as a boy, his first taste of coffee had a similar effect; so did beer, later, and whiskey after that, so he knew what she was going through.

Henry leant outside and took a handful of snow, which he smilingly handed to Mint.

Gratefully, she took it from him and rammed it into her mouth, the coldness of it not seeming to affect her.

Henry laughed out loud, and pretty soon, Mint did too.

They finished eating and Henry drained the last of the coffee as Mint tidied everything away: plates scrubbed with fresh snow, as was the bone spoon and lastly, the coffee pot. She packed them all away and then sat staring at Henry.

He spoke for the first time that day. 'I know you don't understand,' he began, 'but I ain't never been so happy.'

He smiled at her and, although she didn't understand the words, she did understand their meaning.

She reached out and took his hand in both of hers and pressed it warmly to her cheek.

'I don't even know which tribe you come from,' Henry went on, 'or where you've bin or where you was a-headed. Hell, I don't even know if we're gonna make it through this storm or even through winter.

'One thing though,' he added, 'I promise that I'll take real good care o' you.'

He gently squeezed her hands and she responded likewise.

They sat, wrapped in warm clothing, while outside, the blizzard continued throughout the morning. Henry had no idea what time it was or even what day it was – not that that mattered particularly to a trapper – but it was a simple way of staying in touch with both reality and civilization.

The wind began to drop, and the driving snow began to slow a little as the day grew older. Henry guessed it was about noon when it finally died out altogether and, although it was cold, the sky was clear, and the wind was just a thing of the past.

Digging his way out of the shelter, he managed to feed both the mule and the ponies. They'd survived the night standing close to the shelter and to each other, and the thick hide Henry had covered them in was coated with snow, which in effect had kept them even warmer.

The ponies whinnied as Henry approached but the mule seemed to just raise one eye in recognition then lower its head once more.

Now that it was clear, Henry took in the terrain for the first time. He was surrounded by mountains; the trail they'd been following seemed to have been almost completely obliterated by the snow.

He knew he was in a valley, but the fall of snow had been so heavy that it was now hard to distinguish where the valley ended, and the mountains began.

The air felt crisp and clean, and high above, the sun, watery in comparison to the summer months, still shone brightly, and Henry could feel the heat on his face.

Light, reflected up from the pure, white snow almost blinded him in its intensity and he had to squint his eyes almost shut to focus on anything distant.

Mint joined him, her lithe, slim body pressing up close to him, and Henry began to feel himself stir once more. He pulled his thoughts together as he stared ahead.

'We got a mite o' travellin' to do,' he told her. 'Seems like the damn valley's all but filled with snow.'

Mint looked up to his face, watching his lip move and hearing strange words that she tried hard to understand.

Henry pointed ahead, then at himself and finally at Mint. She got the message.

'I gotta scout ahead a-ways,' Henry said, staring into her eyes. He pointed at himself, then he pointed ahead. Then he held her with his good arm and turned her towards the shelter.

'I gotta make sure we can get outta this place. You best stay here,' he said, and pointed at the buffalo-hide that covered the cave entrance that was inches deep in snow.

Mint nodded. She seemed to understand, Henry thought, but he still wondered.

From the travois, which was still laden but free of the pony, Mint brushed snow away, searching for something.

'What're you lookin' for?' Henry asked.

Without answering, Mint turned, a broad smile on her face showing white, perfect teeth. In her hands, she held a pair of snowshoes. She held them out towards Henry, pointing at his feet.

Henry nodded: 'I know where they go,' he said, laughing.

Taking them from her, he took a good look at them. He'd never handled snowshoes before and he marvelled at the handiwork. A willow frame, shaped, Henry thought, like a large salmon, and criss-crossed with an interlacing of rawhide. There were two loose rawhide thongs, one to tie round the instep and the other around the ankle.

By spreading the weight of a man, the snowshoes would stop him sinking thigh-deep into the powdery snow.

'Thanks.' He smiled at her. 'You make these?' Henry worked his fingers as if sewing or knitting, it was all he could think of.

Mint nodded enthusiastically. Pointing at herself and then back at the snowshoes, she smiled and nodded again.

Despite their predicament, Henry couldn't help but notice how her face lit up when she smiled, and he was tempted to just stay put and make love with her all day.

He didn't, though. Although new to the wild, Henry knew they had to find someplace safe to spend the winter. Where they were now was vulnerable to snow slides that could fill this valley up for months, burying them alive in the cave.

Lacing the snowshoes over his moccasins, he stood warily, getting the hang of how to walk with three-foot long snowshoes on.

He soon discovered it wasn't easy. Still having a

tendency to walk quickly, Henry kept tripping up or catching his legs with willow frames, the sound of Mint's laughter his ears and he found it impossible not to join in.

After ten or fifteen minutes, Henry felt confident enough to set off.

Mint had packed his possible sack with provisions and she handed him a Sharps. It wasn't his, and for a second or two he thought about the Hawken rifle, but the breech-loader was a powerful weapon and that might be useful.

Henry had enough nous to realize that grizzlies were hibernating now, so his only natural enemy – apart from Mother Nature herself – were mountain lions.

Making sure he had enough paper cartridges, he searched through his sack, familiarizing himself with its contents. He drew his coat closed, donned his now battered hat, and kissed Mint full on the mouth, unwilling to let her go. Nevertheless, he forced himself to release her and, as he looked into her face he saw tears well but she smiled sweetly up at him and he smiled back.

'I'll be back,' he said, 'just as soon as I can.'

Mint nodded and stepped to one side, allowing him to leave. As he took his first step, she placed the palm of her hand on his cheek, then placed it on her own and finally on her heart.

Henry knew exactly what she was saying, and he did the same thing to her.

Setting off, he turned frequently to wave, and she in turn waved back.

Mint stood rock still outside the small cave until the figure of Henry disappeared, swallowed up by the distance and the blinding brightness.

With a heart as heavy as anything she'd ever felt, Mint turned away and re-entered the cave.

She sat and waited for the return of her man.

TEN

Henry Mullins found the going tough.

The snow, deeply stacked, covered dangers, not least of which in this unknown territory were holes and crevasses.

Although the valley was quite small, the snow painted a different picture, stretching way up high to the mountain tops leaving only the steepest of rises, the jagged rocks, showing through a dark-grey that seemed a total contrast to the blinding white that surrounded them.

The tree-line stopped half-way up the eastern side of the valley and the snow-laden branches, seeming as if the weight of the heavy snowfall would snap them in two, hung low to the ground, destroying the natural shape of the tall, majestic pines.

High above, swirling through the now clear-blue

sky, two eagles soared, seeking prey, their black shapes showing no definition against the backdrop.

As he watched, one of the birds swooped down so quickly that Henry had difficulty focusing. Downwards it plummeted as if out of control, diving to its death.

The giant wings pulled back, acting like a brake just before the bird reached ground level and the eagle appeared to stop momentarily, its giant talons, pointing forwards, took a hold of the unfortunate creature whose life was about to end, and in one swift movement, the bird's legs swung backwards, the deadly talons gripped tight, and a small, white-furred creature, probably a rabbit, took its first flying lesson.

The whole scene played out in total silence, although the killing had taken place less than a hundred yards away, there was no noise from either the bird or its prey.

The eagle lifted effortlessly into the air, flying straight now, heading back to its perch higher up the mountain slopes. No need for it to swoop and swirl any more, just get home to feed itself and its young.

The other bird had flown lower now, circled for a while before following its mate at a safe distance, rather like an army scout keeping an eye open for trouble and ready to defend his family.

The two birds disappeared, leaving nothing moving save the gentle sway of the snow-laden branches.

The silence was deep. As deep as the snow.

Henry stared around the desolate landscape and breathed in the crisp air until he felt his lungs would burst. Then he let the air out slowly, savouring the taste.

Despite his predicament, Henry had lived in the wild long enough to know that whatever happened, he stood a good chance of survival.

The snowshoes were a boon. Without them, Henry knew he'd not have travelled even half the distance. They sank into the snow, but only an inch or two, so it didn't impede his progress any, now that he'd mastered how to walk on them. Taking large, wide strides was the answer. For the first hundred yards or so, Henry had tried to walk normally, but his now-bruised ankles bore testimony to that folly.

With the sun straight ahead, Henry knew he was travelling due east, the sun's rays, although weaker now at the onset of winter, still had warmth and Henry stopped for a while, eyes closed, head raised skywards, feeling the life-giving heat on his face.

It seemed an age ago that he'd left the torrid heat of southern California. The desert, the incessant sun, seemed a dream now, hard to imagine that much heat amongst all this cold.

An involuntary shiver swept across his body even as the sun warmed his face. The clear, crisp air, no dampness like the humidity down south, appeared to dig icy fingers through his clothing, pinpricks of cold.

Henry hunched his shoulders. Even after only a year, he felt the early stages of rheumatism. He'd been warned about it at the rendezvous. All those days spent with wet feet, trapping beaver, the rain soaking through his clothing, drying out over-night, leaving him feeling cold and damp for days on end, beginning to take their toll.

There was no time to dwell on that now though, Henry chided himself. Maybe he'd take better care of himself come Spring. Maybe get a spare set of doeskins when he'd sold his pelts. Maybe even build himself a cabin – for him and Mint – high up, away from everything on two legs.

These thoughts and more, swirled around his head like the eagles had swirled around the sky, with just as much freedom.

Pulling his coat closer, Henry set off once more. He had to make sure there was a way out of the valley that was safe. The last thing he needed now was another snowfall, or worse, an avalanche.

As he neared a wooded area, the creaking and groaning of the branches reached his ears. The sound – the only sound he could hear – seemed deafening as the tortured wood of the living branches fought to maintain a grip on the slender trunks under the weight of the snow.

A gentle breeze that hadn't been apparent out in the open, seemed to swirl through the trees; snow flurries blew here and there. Henry caught them out of the corner of his eye as if a ghost were making its way through the trees, brushing snow off, unseen, as it went.

The scene spooked Henry. Out here in the wild, on land, most of which was untouched and untrodden by man, the only protection you could rely on was the protection you could provide for yourself.

The memory of the grizzly and the attack of the wolf that seemed to stalk him, were still vivid in his mind and made him edgy. In the past twelve months, they had been the only two scary incidents Henry had experienced.

Steeling himself, he followed the lower tree-line eastwards, keeping one eye on the position of the sun and the other searching for any movement.

Trouble was, with even the slightest breeze, branches were moving all the time as if the entire forest were alive.

Henry turned his attention to Mint: breathing deeply through his nose, he could still smell the sweetness of her body, the tang of her long, silky-black hair as it brushed across his face. A warmth, generating upwards from his groin, swept over his body and a thin smile appeared on his face. It was all he could do to stop himself shouting out in happiness.

In that instant, Henry decided that the cabin was no 'maybe' – it was a definite. He'd build them a home they'd spend the rest of their lives in.

For the first time since leaving the south, Henry had plans. He'd still hunt and trap, but he now felt a sense of purpose. There was a reason for living now, a reason for trapping, other than for himself.

The sun had long reached its zenith and was now racing westwards as if the winter cold was making it hurry home.

The crisp air became noticeably colder and the wind strengthened. No more a gentle breeze, gusts of icy-cold air assailed Henry as he trudged, head bent, into the wind.

Clouds that only an hour or so ago didn't exist, scudded across the sky, being lifted by the mountains and Henry could hear the snow in them growing as the colder air way up high began to freeze the moisture content.

Henry's first experience of both cold and snow had been exciting, it almost brought out the boy in him as he watched the first tentative snowfalls. But now, after only a week, he began to realize that the cold was just as much a killer here as the heat had been down south – maybe worse. At least in the heat you could find someplace to cool down in, but out in the cold there was little respite.

The tingling Henry felt in his feet was becoming painful. He knew his toes were freezing up and if he didn't try and do something about it soon, he'd not be able to continue.

Resting up, Henry rooted through his possible sack. He found two bandannas, not very thick, but he double- and triple-folded them to wrap around his feet and ankles. Over these he tied strips of doeskin to help keep them in place and insulate against the cold and wet snow.

A faint mist was rising as the watery heat of the sun began to cool down as dusk approached. The air became moist and the cold was chilling, seeping through to Henry's bones.

Before replacing his makeshift gloves, Henry blew on his white-tipped fingers and rubbed his hands up and down his trouser legs. The tingling in his fingers turned to sharp pain as feeling began to return. The whiteness disappeared, and the calloused fingers turned a bright-red, pain throbbing through in unison with his heartbeat.

Wrapping his neckerchief over his mouth and nose, Henry resealed his possible sack and donned his gloves. His body felt strangely numb and lacklustre, as if his energy was being sapped, movement became an effort and he shook his head to try and clear his brain.

With eyes burning from strain at the constant glare of the blindingly white snow, Henry moved on.

The snowshoes began to feel heavy, each step suddenly becoming an effort of will as the muscles in his legs began to scream out with overwork.

This was a totally new experience for Henry, and he even had time to try work out what was happening to him. He knew he needed to find shelter – and fast – otherwise he was about to freeze to death.

The suddenness of the drop in temperature was startling; one minute he was reasonably comfortable and the next, chilled to the bone.

Through aching eyes, Henry squinted at the smooth, unending blanket of snow that covered up even the most rugged of land. He could see no other place to rest up than in the woods and that thought didn't exactly cheer him.

Henry veered to his left, almost without thinking, and headed into the wooded area. The wind here seemed to be swirling less, the snow being blown off the branches reduced visibility, but only in patches.

He had to light a fire. If he didn't, Henry felt he'd freeze to death.

As he kicked through the snow, looking for anything that would burn, he came across a small hollow where the action of the wind had scooped out enough snow to leave it almost bare.

To one side was a thick bank of snow that towered up some seven or eight feet, giving quite a bit of shelter from the now rapidly increasing wind. The hollow was still strewn with dead branches and as Mint had packed some tinder in his possible sack, Henry knew he'd get a fire going.

Henry recalled the old trappers telling him never to fall asleep in the snow. Sleep in snow, die in snow.

Stepping down into the hollow, he gathered as much timber as he could manage and built a stack by the snow bank. Sitting, he could feel no wind at all.

Opening his sack once more, Henry brought out the tinder, dried moss from the cave and small twigs, all tied up neatly with a strip of doeskin.

Arranging the branches like a teepee, Henry placed the tinder in the centre as he'd seen Mint do and then rooted out his matches.

He struggled with the matchstick as his fingers, although warmer and with some feeling in them, felt as if they belonged to somebody else. Eventually, the match caught.

The tinder flared up and the brightness of the flames was the first indication Henry had of both colour and impending nightfall. So intent had he been on finding shelter, he'd failed to notice the light going.

Making sure the fire caught, Henry peered around the murkiness of his shelter. The top of the snow bank was a bluish-white now as the sun sank in the west. The long, black shadows thrown down by the trees, now rested on blue snow as the moon took over from the sun, its light cold and unwelcoming.

A harbinger of the night to come, Henry thought as he settled himself by the fire. The heat was thin yet welcome. The damp wood sent up a spiral of white smoke that was swept away by the wind as soon as it topped the hollow.

Night fell like a stone down a well; one second it seemed twilight, the next, blackness, the only light being shed by the orange-red glow of the fire as it fought to stay alive.

In the distance, Henry heard the familiar baying

of wolves or coyotes; he could sense their presence, he could even picture the animals standing atop a rocky ledge, howling to the full moon.

Henry shivered again, but this time, it wasn't the cold.

ELEVEN

Using two branches, Henry fashioned a shelter. It wouldn't shield him from the wind, neither would it deter any predator; if it snowed heavily during the night it would probably collapse, but the psychological impact of having something over his head, other than his battered hat, was uplifting.

As the now dark clouds scudded across an even darker sky, the moon shone intermittently through the gaping holes, sending a harsh, silver light reflecting off the snow, then it was back to blackness.

Henry was careful not to stare into the friendly flames of the campfire for too long. He needed his night vision and the flames seemed to draw his eyes to it as if mesmerized, so that when he looked up again it was as black as all hell itself.

Hands and feet were warming now, the pain had subsided and the all too familiar tingling sensation filled his limbs. Aches and pains and cramps racked his body as his temperature built up slowly, but only on the front side. Only the side directly facing the campfire felt the benefit. His back was freezing and becoming stiff.

Shifting position, Henry sat with his sore arm nearest the fire; he felt the side of his neck tingle as the heat penetrated cold skin. He couldn't see, but Henry was sure his skin had turned blue where the heat didn't hit.

Food!

The thought hit him like a bullet from a buffalo rifle. His guts were screaming at him for food. He'd been so intent on keeping awake and getting warmer that fuel for the inner body had completely slipped his dulled mind.

Removing his gloves, he untied his possible sack and began rooting round inside.

Mint, he knew, had packed enough food to keep him going until he either found a way out or trapped something fresh. Water wasn't a problem. He scooped up a couple of handfuls of snow and dumped it in a tin pot and sat it directly on the flames. Even then, he sat idly watching the snow melt until bubbles began to dance from the centre of the pot and burst on the surface, sending a thin, watery cloud of steam rising into the air a few inches before the cold snapped it like a dead branch off a dying tree.

What little coffee he had left, he split into two and threw it into the boiling water.

The smell hit his nostrils like a spring trap closing on a deer's leg. His mouth watered and, using a twig, he stirred the brew to hurry it along.

Within five minutes of scooping up the snow, Henry had his first mouthful of coffee. It shot down his throat like the rough brandy his ex-landlady had given him once when he came down with a heavy cold.

He felt it hit his stomach and as it did so, generated warmth that seemed to fill his entire body.

The wind howled, sending up a fine spray of already-fallen snow that inched in and around Henry's campsite. A fine layer of snow already covered his makeshift shelter and from beneath it, Henry gave it a poke to dislodge the snow before it dislodged his shelter.

Now he grinned. He'd survive the night, of that he was sure. Though he wasn't sure why he was sure, he just knew it.

The cold had come as a shock, it had taken him by surprise and he'd almost floundered. As Henry sat sipping at his second cup of watery coffee, he recollected that, just as the sun began to sink, so had his mind; his will seemed to seep out of him, leaving him feeling that sleep was the only answer to his problems.

He grinned again.

Mother Nature wasn't going to get him tonight. He'd learned a valuable lesson: camp up well before the sun goes down.

Bringing out a strip of jerky, Henry bit into it hungrily. That and the coffee had revived his senses enough for him to turn his thoughts to Mint. Dear, sweet little Mint.

His head was filled with visions of their lovemaking during the past few nights. The smell of her hair filled his nostrils and he could even feel the silky smoothness of her body. An even warmer glow washed over him, warmer than both fire and hot coffee could produce, and his head almost went into a spin.

Henry Mullins was in love. He was in love with an Indian girl he couldn't even speak to, but love it was.

The cooked beaver tail and pemmican cakes never tasted better and Henry felt strength flow through his veins, pushing the killer cold out of his body.

Howling coyotes echoed in the distance. At least, Henry thought they were coyotes. The vision of those cruel, yellow eyes that had stared directly into his as the vicious fangs had sunk into his arm made Henry shiver.

He could smell the musky odour of the animal even now, above the aroma of the coffee, and fear gripped his belly for an instant.

He pulled himself together, grabbing hold of the Sharps for comfort. The cold of the metal burned his fingers as he gripped it tightly, forcing him to let go and lean the barrel on his shoulder.

A grin, more like a smirk, crossed his face. 'Come on,' he said out loud. 'I'm ready for you!'

Nothing answered his voice. The wind still howled, blowing wisps of snow every which way, hissing as some landed in the campfire.

The baying continued, paying no heed to Henry. Snow began to fall, lightly at first, but the sky was full, and Henry knew it was more than just a flurry.

Large snowflakes obliterated his vision, the fire began to die down and Henry wished he'd built it under the shelter instead of out in the open.

He piled on more wood, knowing he'd have to keep it up all night. Either that, or he'd freeze to death.

The wind grew stronger and the snow began to

sting his face. Already, the area around the fire, which had been steaming moments before, had a fine coating of fresh snow and the bright leaping flames were under constant attack.

Henry pulled his coat tighter, the howling wind seemed to chill him, and the feeling of well-being began to slip again. To add to his shelter, Henry rammed the snowshoes, point first, into the snow. Almost immediately, the hide-strip webbing began to fill with snow and, within five minutes, the shoes disappeared and in their place was a wall of webbing which took the sting out of the wind.

Rooting out his possible sack from beneath a pile of snow, Henry pulled out the Indian pony-blanket. He wrapped it around his shoulders and head and left the sacking over his legs. All the while, he tried his damnedest to keep the fire alight, but he could see he was fighting a losing battle.

His earlier confidence of beating Mother Nature and surviving the night, rapidly began to ebb away and a form of utter helplessness descended on him.

It was a full-blown blizzard.

Snow was piling up faster and faster; first around the tree-trunks, then gradually spreading as the wind painted a fresh canvas of white, obliterating everything.

Pulling his hat down harder, trying to shield his

eyes, Henry knew he was in for the toughest fight of his life.

The enemy?

The weather.

Mint was faring better.

Inside the small cave, she was as snug as a bug. The wind rattled through the blanket she'd covered the entrance with, but the heat from the campfire warmed the entire cave.

She didn't feel the cold as much as Henry – years spent living in the wild had seen to that.

She'd already cooked and eaten her evening meal and was arranging the buffalo hides for her bed when faint rumbles could be felt through the rock floor.

Mint stiffened.

She remained stock-still on all fours as the vibration built up. At first, she feared an earthquake. She'd heard of the gods showing their displeasure by shaking sense into the world, from her grandfather, but never actually felt it before.

Small stones and a pile of dust fell from the cave roof and Mint feared the whole thing would come down on top of her.

The noise grew louder, nearer.

Then she realized what it was.

Avalanche!

The ground shook violently, and the faraway rumble grew to a growl. She could hear, above all the noise, the rending of tree trunks, as if matchsticks.

Mint sank back to the rear of the cave, covering herself with the buffalo hides she was about to go to sleep in.

She prayed to her gods and waited.

The noises outside continued for several minutes before a deathly calm descended. Even the wind seemed to drop, adding to the eerie calmness.

Mint coughed, her lungs full of dust, her mouth full of grit. But there was no echo. The cough was swallowed up in her tomb.

Fearing the worst, Mint crawled forward, past the campfire, towards the blanket and rawhide she'd fixed over the cave entrance.

For several seconds her hand rested on the makeshift door before, taking a deep breath, she pulled it open.

What greeted her made her hold her breath. What she saw made her grab her amulet, her good luck charm, and she began to chant, softly.

Henry Mullins thought he must have dropped off to sleep for the distant rumble made his eyes shoot wide open. He could feel a slight tremor in the ground and he, too, thought he was in the middle of an earthquake.

He'd lived through one before, feeling totally helpless as a child, as the ground shook and rattled beneath his feet, making it almost impossible to stand. He'd watched as his house had collapsed like a pack of cards. He'd seen great fissures open in the ground ready to swallow him whole. He'd stayed on all fours for minutes on end, praying the shaking would stop.

When it did, Henry, a boy of six maybe seven, stared wide-eyed at what used to be his home, his security, the only place he'd ever known.

Then he began to scream. He screamed the names of his parents, over and over and over, until he was hoarse, until he thought his throat was red-raw and he could feel the blood running into his mouth.

It was Henry who'd found them; it was Henry who'd dug them out with his bare, young hands.

These images came and disappeared quicker than Henry could blink. The slight tremor in the ground seemed to have released these long-buried thoughts which came back vividly, as if they'd only happened yesterday.

Henry wiped his eyes. He wasn't sure if it was

snow or tears that temporarily blinded him.

Above the howling wind, Henry heard the roar and crackle coming some distance behind him.

Behind him!

The thought hit him between the eyes like a tomahawk, his scalp tensed as he realized what the noise could be.

He'd heard tales of avalanches, back at the last rendezvous. The old-timers had told him to look for the signs: a heavy snowfall, bright sunshine during the day, then a freeze. Partial melting of the fresh snow, then even fresher snow on top of that, and plenty of it.

They'd told him stories of whole mountain forests being devastated by the charging snow. Some of the trappers had likened it to a herd of wild buffalo stampeding across the prairie, the rumble of thousands of hoofs; the destruction of anything and everything in their path.

Henry shivered. It wasn't the cold. He was only glad the avalanche hadn't hit him.

The significance of that earlier thought. Behind him! Mint!

TWELVE

Henry built up the campfire as best he could. The wood, covered in snow, hissed and sent plumes of steam into the cold night air, which were devoured eagerly by the freezing wind.

Henry's resolve and purpose were set now. Mint could be in danger. Mint could be d— No, he wouldn't even think that word, let alone imagine the consequences of it.

He had to stay alive. He had to survive. If Mint was in trouble, he had to get back to her, make sure she was all right.

Frustration bit into him. He wanted to leave now, to backtrack, to find the cave.

Henry knew that was foolish. He knew he'd die for sure if he even tried it.

Sleep was impossible now anyway, he thought,

and managed a grin.

'You ain't killin' me!' he shouted into the wind. 'You ain't takin' me yet!'

The effort of shouting seemed to warm him. It filled him with courage. He pulled the buffalo hide tighter round his body. Poked more snow off the shelter, which had already begun to sag dangerously low over his head, and with a look of grim determination, sat staring straight ahead into the windswept snowstorm that played out all around him.

The distant howling of wolves had ceased. The moon, unseen now through the dark clouds, failed to get its spooky light to the ground. It was pitch black.

Henry sat and waited.

A blood-red light lit up the valley. It jumped over the tree-line to the east and swept down on to the valley floor like lava from a volcano. Henry's eyes watched it as it crawled towards him. Warmth seemed to flood through his body even before the early morning rays hit him.

He blinked. His eyelids felt frozen. They didn't belong to him, for he couldn't feel them. He couldn't feel his face, either, or his hands. His feet were miles away, out of sight and nothing to do with him.

The rawhide was stiff. Beneath the coating of

snow that had managed to cling to the matted fur despite the attempts of the howling gale to dislodge them, a coating of ice had formed, and it shattered as Henry moved his arms in an attempt to get himself free from the icy grip.

Pulling the rawhide off, Henry then tried to kick off the blanket that covered his legs, but his legs refused to do as they were told.

Stretching his arms out high and wide, Henry felt his shoulder joints crack; then his elbows and wrists. His hands, which had gripped the inside of the rawhide so tightly all night, were like the talons of a golden eagle. He stared at his claw-like fingers and, one by one, he opened them up.

He didn't recognize the terrain. The snow had done a good job. There were no tracks to follow, a blanket of white covered the ground, reflecting the sunlight stronger and stronger as the sun rose.

The campfire was dead. Despite his efforts to keep it alive, the snow had closed around it leaving a small circle of blackened ground.

Henry thrust his hands under his armpits and waggled his fingers, trying to get some feeling back. He needed his hands for his legs. He needed his legs to find Mint!

The hots arrived as the blood forced its way through constricted veins and arteries. Down his

120

arms and into his fingers. The throbbing was unbearable, and even while in such pain, Henry knew that when it subsided, he'd have to go through the whole rigmarole again to get his legs and feet in working order.

His doeskins were as stiff as a board and he felt as if he'd been hung out to dry.

Slowly, feeling returned to his fingers: the whiteness replaced by red in his fingertips. Grabbing hold of the blanket that covered his legs, Henry tugged it off. It took two or three attempts as his fingers didn't have the strength yet, but he knew they would soon.

He started rubbing on his upper thighs, pushing his hands hard up and down from his groin to his knees. He shifted his feet, not even an inch, but enough to know they were his.

Reaching into his possible sack, he brought out the last of his tinder. Working like an old man, stiff and shaky, he arranged the tinder and placed a few damp twigs over it like a teepee. The match was a harder prospect.

Try as he might, his fingers wouldn't grip the small wooden shaft of the match. Every time he thought he had it, he dropped it. Despite the chill, sweat broke out on his forehead as frustration took over once more.

Then he had it. Gripped tight between thumb and forefinger, he struck the match with his other thumb and it caught first time. It was a good job the wind had died with the dawn, as it took Henry a few seconds to manoeuvre the flame towards the tinder. The moss and dried leaves lapped the offered flame greedily and the damp twigs began to steam.

Now he had heat, the fire and the sun, Henry began to feel better. He certainly didn't look better. His hat and eyebrows were covered with snow and his blond beard had icicles hanging off the end of it.

He rubbed his face hard with both hands, feeling the tingling in his cheeks. He felt his snow- and ice-sodden beard and, despite his predicament, decided it had to come off. It was time Mint saw his face.

Scooping up snow, he dumped it in his pan and waited for it to boil. While he waited, he began cutting. His knife, ever sharp, cut through the tangled mat with ease, until he had an even growth of less than half an inch.

As the water began to bubble, Henry took the pan off the flames and, using a clean bandanna, he soaked his face with the hot water. It felt good, real good. Then he set to work with his knife, careful not to cut himself too much.

122

Without a looking-glass, it wasn't an easy task, and, as far as he was aware, he hadn't cut himself up too badly in the process.

His whole face tingled now, the hot water and the cold air saw to that, but he felt a damn sight better and hoped he looked it too.

With no coffee left, Henry drank what was left of the boiled water; it slaked his thirst, but he sure wished the water had coffee in it. He bit off a hunk of jerky, packed his possible bag while he chewed, and then proceeded to stand up for the first time in fourteen hours.

Mint had no idea how thick the snow wall that greeted her was. She could see pine cones and twigs embedded in the white wall and, as it was lighter in the cave than it was outdoors anyway, she could see nothing of the outside world.

She squatted on her haunches and pondered her situation: should she start to dig her way out? She thought not. It might worsen her plight. Besides, where would she put the snow she'd dug out? The cave was small, there was no room. At least inside, she was warm.

Mint turned her gaze to the campfire. It burned brightly. The small wisps of smoke rose steadily into the air and disappeared. This gave her heart, if the smoke was getting out then the air must be getting in!

At least, she thought, I won't suffocate.

She had enough food to last a month, maybe more, and water was no problem: if she used the wood sparingly, wrapped herself in the buffalo hides, she would survive. She knew 'Hearney' would come for her.

There was nothing she could do now. When dawn broke, she might be able to see something through the snow wall, but she had no idea how thick it was or what else might be embedded in it. Waiting for Spring was not an option she would consider.

Mint decided to keep herself busy. First, by tidying up the cave floor, gathering all the wood she could and making a store. Then, she'd go through the food-sack, mentally noting each day's allowance, then reducing it further to eke out as many days as she could.

If she lit the fire only at night, it would last longer. The thought then struck her that if she was entombed for many days, she would have difficulty remembering when it was daytime and when it was night time.

Mint arranged the buffalo hides into a pile in the centre of the cave right next to the fire. She studied the roof carefully, checking for loose stones and looking to see if she could see where the fresh air was coming from, but the shadows were too dense to make anything out properly.

What she did find was a branch big enough to be used to make a torch.

Tearing strips of cloth, she bound them securely to one end of the branch and then smeared buffalo fat all over the cloth. The torch lit straight away and for the first time Mint was able to check the cave out thoroughly.

The roof sloped from front to back: near the cave entrance, it was only five feet off the ground, but back at the rear, Mint estimated it went as high as a teepee.

There didn't appear to be any loose debris on the roofline that she could make out, neither could she see any chinks of light. However, it was night time and if the avalanche had passed over the cave then light wouldn't get through anyway.

Making sure there were no hibernating creatures sharing the cave with her, Mint doused the torch; she might be in need of it later.

The light from the dying campfire lit the cave well enough for a while, so Mint decided to add a few more pieces of wood and then sleep.

*

On legs that felt like jelly, Henry dragged himself to his feet. His head swam, and he felt slightly dizzy. He had no idea a night in these sub-zero temperatures could have such an effect on the human body.

It was as if all the strength had been sapped out of his muscles by the cold during the night. Even now, with the watery heat from the sun shining high above, he felt as cold as ice.

An involuntary shiver swept down his back as if someone had just walked over his grave. Or he'd walked over someone else's.

For as far as the eye could see, all Henry could see was white. There was the odd rocky outcrop that had managed to shrug off the blanket of snow during the night, but everything was coated.

The reflected light from the sun made Henry's eyes water and he had to squint until his eyes were damn-near closed. Yet he could still feel that glare burning into his eyeballs.

What Henry had thought would be his salvation – the daylight, sun, surviving the bitterly-cold night – was proving just as dangerous.

He couldn't focus.

Then he heard the snuffles of creatures close by – and they sure didn't sound like jackrabbits.

A low growl – almost inaudible – came from behind him. Henry spun around, his newly-acquired Sharps at the ready, but he saw nothing.

Then, again from behind, he heard another growl, a deep-throated growl that lasted nearly twenty seconds.

Then he heard growls and slobbering that seemed to come from all around him. Yet still Henry could see nothing except the white.

Raising the rifle, he loosed two shots into the air.

The growling ceased abruptly.

In the eerie silence that followed, nothing seemed to move at all. Even the wind had died down to such an extent that the occasional snow flurry, whipped up from the ground or down from the trees, halted.

The growling took up again.

It seemed closer this time and Henry knew he was surrounded.

There was no place to hide, no place to run. Henry stood in the middle of a desolate landscape with not even a nearby rock to protect his backside.

With his arm still throbbing from the previous attack down by the river – an attack that now seemed a lifetime ago – his shooting was hampered by the sling, but he didn't have the strength in his arm yet to lift the rifle. Gripping the ice-cold barrel with two fingers and a thumb, Henry cocked the Sharps with his right hand and waited.

The growling stopped once more, and a bark broke the steely air and almost made Henry jump out of his skin.

His trigger-finger tugged and a shot sank silently into the snow, only the crash of the explosion as it left the chamber made any impact, the snow merely closed over the tiny hole near his feet where the slug had entered.

Gripping the barrel once more in his left hand, Henry tried to cock the weapon again. This time he met resistance.

The lever-action wouldn't move. A slug was stuck in the chamber.

Using what little strength he had, Henry tried to do with one arm what he really needed two to do, but the lever-action stayed put.

Henry was defenceless.

THIRTEEN

From out of nowhere, three wolves appeared, jaws wide showing yellow fangs that seemed to glisten as they slobbered in anticipation.

Their growling was deafening as they stalked Henry slowly, getting closer and closer and braver and braver as hunger drove them on.

Henry gripped the rifle in his right hand by the long barrel. If he couldn't fire the damn thing, he thought as the animals neared, he'd sure go down fighting.

Instead of circling, which was what Henry thought they'd do, the three wolves came towards him more or less in line. Henry could see their yellow and black eyes boring into his; their grey fur standing on end down their spines, heads low and menacing, tails even lower.

The lead dog moved towards Henry's left leg, never taking its eyes off Henry's; the other two seemed to stand off some, waiting to see what would happen, and ready to pounce.

Henry spread his legs wide and dug the snowshoes in deeper to attain as much balance as he could. He knew that, should the dogs pounce and he fell, it would all be over. He wouldn't stand a chance. He had to keep on his feet.

Still growling, its fangs bared, saliva dripping from its lips, the lead dog seemed to hesitate, trying to make up its made which way to attack.

That was Henry's opening. He had to turn defence into attack. Bringing the wooden stock of the rifle down in a smooth arc, he caught the wolf on the side of the head, taking the animal by surprise.

Blood spurted immediately from a gash just below the wolf's left ear, staining the virgin-white snow a brilliant scarlet before it spread and sank in, becoming a dull red.

For a moment or two, the wolf looked bewildered. Then slowly, it staggered and swayed, its legs buckled, and the wolf sank gently to the ground, panting. It didn't roll over and die, which was what Henry was hoping for; it merely seemed to be taking a breather.

The growling ceased from the other two dogs. As the stock hit the lead dog, they jumped from all fours into the air and backed off, tails between their legs. They growled in a show of bravado, then began barking, but not for long, their bravery evaporating as hunger took hold once more. In front of them they saw food. They stood, keeping a wary eye on Henry and waited to see what their leader would do next.

The answer was, nothing.

The now dying dog's head sank slowly into the snow and its eyes closed. As Henry watched, he could still see the animal's chest moving, breathing in and out. Blood was still oozing from the wound on its head and the smell must have filled the nostrils of the other two dogs.

Without any warning, they both leapt upon their erstwhile leader, tearing great lumps of fur off the prone body with their powerful jaws and fangs. They took not the slightest notice of Henry. The downed dog didn't move as it was being devoured and Henry felt a little sorry for the beast, despite the fact that, given the chance, it would have been him lying there.

The law of the wild prevailed. The animals were hungry, with game being scarce in the winter months, and Mother Nature decreed there was no love lost in any species. It was eat to stay alive or be eaten.

Henry backed off slowly. He didn't want to disturb the two remaining wolves as they gorged themselves on one of their own. He certainly didn't want to remind them of his presence. Steam rose into the air as guts were ripped free of the body and the two wolves seemed to swallow everything without chewing.

The area around the feeding frenzy was scarlet with blood and gore. Then the two surviving wolves seemed to turn their attention on each other.

As Henry quietly left the scene, it became obvious the two dogs were fighting over the entrails.

They rolled and growled and fought with even more gusto than that which they'd displayed when attacking the third dog, and Henry felt safe enough to move off at a quicker pace.

High above, out of the corner of his eye, Henry caught the dark shape of an eagle. He doubted the bird had smelled blood, but, with its keen eyesight, it could probably see it.

Eagles weren't that fond of dead meat, preferring to kill, but food – any food – was better than nothing.

The graceful bird circled lower and lower, its wings not beating as it seemed to slide through the air, the two fighting wolves didn't even notice as the eagle landed, and its powerful beak ripped off some fur- and blood-coated flesh and departed again in the blink of an eye.

The two wolves stopped their fighting as they heard the whoosh of the eagle's wings as it took to the air and safety. Both animals just stood and stared, heads cocked to one side and, for a second, they both looked harmless if quizzical, and Henry was reminded of the old dog he'd had as a kid.

However, that impression didn't last long as both dogs returned to the carcase and resumed filling their bellies before anything else came along to deprive them of their meal.

Henry carried on. He'd stopped shaking now – just – and Mint returned to his thoughts.

He scanned ahead, hoping to see something he recognised, some sign, but all he could pinpoint were the mountains to his right. The snowstorm of the previous night had wiped out all his tracks and even where he'd left a rock or two as a guide, there was nothing.

The valley floor was crisscrossed with the tracks of small animals, mainly jackrabbits, as they scavenged for food, but of his own, nothing.

It was mid-morning and the breeze began to freshen, almost imperceptibly at first, but the telltale swirls of snow being blown up began to get bigger and more common.

Henry froze – quite literally – when a dull thud sounded off to his left. As he turned, the branches of a pine were still shaking in the after-effects of losing a pile of snow. The green of the needles seeming unreal after staring for so long at virtually nothing but white.

The cold was beginning to bite into Henry's bones again as he trudged headlong into the wind. The snow flurries attacked his face, rather like the desert sands in a sandstorm, and he felt as if a layer of his skin was being rubbed off by the churning ice.

For a minute or two he had to stand rock-still as the wind whipped up the snow around his feet and almost blinded him; he felt as if he was in the middle of a localized blizzard.

It became harder to discern where the land finished, and sky began. The air was full of snow and what light the watery sun had managed to shed was rapidly disappearing behind huge snow clouds that filled the sky.

Henry knew more snow was imminent and that if he didn't find cover . . . well, he knew the answer to that.

He stared around the utter desolation of the valley that he imagined, in the summer would be a glorious place to spend some time, hunting, fishing maybe. But now, all it held was death.

It was as he was scanning the terrain Henry began to feel that something wasn't quite right. He rubbed at his eyes: they felt, to his ungloved fingers, cold and alien to him. He looked down at his hands and saw nothing!

Stumbling almost blindly, panic filling him as he realized all he could see was a white, blindingly bright light but very little definition. Using the rifle to steady himself, Henry kept walking in what he assumed was the right direction.

With the swirling wind getting stronger by the minute, it was impossible to gauge whether he was walking in a straight line or merely wandering around in circles.

Lifting his head high, Henry tried to make out the skyline, but again, all he saw was a whiteness that seemed to drill straight into his brain, dulling his senses.

Shelter was now his main concern. He remembered the snow-filled sky and, with the wind building up, he knew that when it did snow again, it would be a blizzard.

It was as these thoughts were flooding through his mind that he felt something brush against the side of his leg.

Henry stopped walking. Eyes wide open, trying to see what it was, was like staring at a freshly-painted clapboard from close up.

He felt the touch again, it was gentle, a nudge.

Henry leant forwards and tried to feel what it was brushing his leg.

His cold hand rested on matted fur.

Henry pulled his arm back as if it was about to be snapped off in a bear trap. Without proper eyesight, he had no idea what the creature was. Then logic took over. If the animal, whatever it was, had meant him harm, it could have attacked him freely and there wasn't a damn thing Henry could have done about it.

Maybe it was a mutt, he thought, some tamed dog that got lost or something.

'Here, boy,' Henry said. 'Don't be afraid.'

There was no sound from the animal and Henry lost touch with it, although he did manage to make out a slightly darker shape to one side of him.

'Come on, boy,' Henry called again in a softer voice.

This time, the brush against his right leg was longer, as if the animal were rubbing its head.

Henry knelt. He knew he was taking a chance, but with practically no eyesight and a blizzard blowing up, he had no choice.

The animal licked Henry's face and he smelled the fetid breath of the animal: a meat eater, of that he was certain.

'Come on now, boy,' he said soothing, rubbing the animal's ears, 'let's see if you an' me can find some shelter afore the snow comes.'

There was a bark, a friendly bark, and Henry knew then it was a dog.

'There's a good boy,' Henry went on. 'Let's find us a nice hidey-hole till this blows over.'

The animal walked on, Henry stood and, keeping one hand on its back, followed.

The animal's pace was slow, and Henry instinctively knew the dog was leading him to safety.

The wind was howling and whistling through the distant trees and then the snow began to fall. Large cold flakes hit Henry in the face, almost horizontally as the gale blew towards him. Still they walked on until Henry walked into a snow bank and, despite the snowshoes, fell backwards, rolling ten feet back before he came to a halt.

Within seconds, the dog's snout was in Henry's face, licking at his cheek.

'I'm OK, fella,' Henry said, and got to his feet. 'Just give me a little more warnin' next time.'

He followed the dog up the incline until he reached the snow bank again. This time he stopped short of it as the fingers of his right hand touched the cold surface.

He could hear scampering and digging and the snow beneath his feet began to pile up. The dog was digging into the bank, piling the snow round Henry. Every few minutes, Henry lifted first one foot and then the other to keep free.

'That's a boy,' Henry kept saying encouragingly as the animal continued to dig away at the snow bank, and Henry could hear the scraping as the dog's paws clawed at the snow.

Then, there came a voice.

It seemed to come directly in front of Henry – from out of the snow bank.

FOURTEEN

The cold, lack of sleep for the past thirty-six hours and the throbbing in his arm, began to take its toll on Henry Mullins.

His abortive foray into the valley had cost him dearly. He tried vainly to keep his eyes from closing, but exhaustion got the better of him.

Still blinded by the snow, Henry sank to his knees. He could hear the scratching and digging of the dog and just make out a vague shape against the white backdrop, but that was the last thing he saw before falling face first into a cold cushion of snow.

Henry wasn't sure if he was unconscious, asleep or just plain dreaming, but he seemed to be aware of all that was going on around him. The howling wind, the snow being forced through the air, stinging his exposed skin like a hail of bullets; the unrelenting as the gale-force winds passed over rocks and through branches, whipping up as much snow as it deposited.

Did he hear the voice again? Henry concentrated, concentrated hard, but wasn't sure. Maybe, he thought, I am dreaming. Maybe I just want to hear that voice, that sweet voice calling out to me, beckoning me to a safer place.

The sun shone brightly overhead as Henry rode through the desert. Ahead of him he saw dunes and cactus and tumbleweed. He could feel the heat of the sun on his face as it burned through him.

Then he realized that, in his dream-like state, the heat that Henry thought he could feel was, in fact, the cold of the snow.

He tried desperately to lift his face away from the burning cold, but his strength was gone and with it, the will to survive. Sleep. Henry wanted sleep more than anything else in the world.

His brain seemed to be turning to mush. All the advice on survival he'd gleaned from the old-time trappers at the rendezvous meant nothing in these circumstances.

Sleep was all that mattered. If he could sleep, maybe he'd wake up refreshed, stronger, able to continue.

The winds whipped around his body and snow

began to pile up over him. All the while, he could faintly hear a voice calling his name and the sound of the dog frantically digging.

Then he heard nothing. Even before his eyes firmly closed, his hearing had gone and Henry fell into a death-sleep.

From inside the warm cave, Mint could hear faint scratching noises rising over the sound of the wind.

At first, all she had thoughts on was Henry coming back to rescue her. Nothing else seemed to matter. But her senses, inherited from past generations, told her not to be so gullible.

Outside, there could be a bear lurking, disturbed from its winter sleep by the avalanche and now looking for somewhere else to hibernate.

It could be wolves, with their keen sense of smell, trying to dig their way in and attack her and eat whatever they could scavenge.

Mint calmed herself down, and reached into the large leather pouch that had belonged to her dead grandfather and took out his tomahawk.

The wooden handle, still bearing the sweat stains of the man who was the last of her family, felt reassuring in her small hands as she gripped it tightly.

Blood still stained the carved stone head of the tomahawk, testimony to the many battles her tribe had fought – both with other tribes and the ever-encroaching pale-faces.

Tied to the top of the shaft with deer-skin hung two eagle feathers, symbolic of the position her grandfather had held in the tribe.

The sounds of digging grew louder and with it, the noise of the howling gales outside. Mint shivered. She would defend her life and her possessions to the limit, of that she was certain. She also knew, way back in her memory, that if it was a bear, the tomahawk would be of little use.

Crouched by the cave entrance, she waited to see what fate had in store for her.

No more than thirty feet away from the slowly-freezing body of Henry Mullins, two wolves stood, peering with dark-yellow eyes at the scene being played out before them. One thing and one thing only, was on their feral minds – food – because food meant survival.

Still, their fear of the other dog, and the uncertainty of their position and mistrust of each other, held them back. Their stomachs told them to attack, their brains told them otherwise.

The scent of the man lying in the snow, filled their nostrils almost to distraction, but they were young and uncertain of their own capabilities.

They knew they had to eat, eat anything, yet neither animal knew what to do next.

The large dog that was digging through the snow sensed their presence and stopped. Raising his head, it sniffed the air, despite the howling wind; it caught their scent and recognized it immediately.

Staring through the snow, the animal fixed its deadly gaze on the two wolves. Its mouth open, fangs exposed, it let out a low growl of warning that was whipped away by the wind.

Turning slowly, never taking its eyes off the other two animals, it faced them.

The two wolves moved slightly apart, blood still covered their snouts from their previous kill and they knew that in order to eat, they'd have to fight and kill their old leader, the animal that they'd followed for most of their short lives.

Circling, keeping their distance, the two wolves made their move. The older, more experienced dog stood his ground, there would be no rash move made by him.

With Henry's body as the centre, the two younger wolves, each one snarling, fangs bared, the hair down their spine standing on edge like a razor-back pig.

Slowly, they began to edge their way forward; each dog keeping a watchful eye on the other; the

143

older dog turning his head from left to right in slow, mechanical movements.

He seemed unworried as the two wolves closed to within ten feet either side of him. His thick, strong legs were planted firmly in the snow; he let out a blood-curdling yowl, which made the two younger wolves halt in their tracks.

Doubt entered their minds – briefly – before hunger took control once more and both growled in response, but their growl was timid by comparison.

Nevertheless, they edged forward once more, closing the gap between themselves and their prey in inches, rather than feet.

Again, their progress was halted, as the old dog, who'd been in more tight corners than his adversaries had caught buck-rabbits, growled. This time the growl was low-pitched and menacing.

A rush of blood, pangs of hunger, who knows what prompted one of the wolves to make a move. He darted forward seeing only the exposed neck of the older dog.

But he wasn't quick enough or careful enough. The old campaigner stood his ground and his vicious fangs clamped on to the neck of the on-rushing animal in a vice-like grip that only death would release.

144

A high-pitched howl escaped the younger wolf's mouth, a short howl, as oxygen was cut off; the dog could neither breathe in or out.

Instead of joining the attack, the other inexperienced wolf stood and watched, biding his time. It seemed to him that, either way, there would be food available. Little did he realize that, if he'd attacked right then, not only would there be wolf meat to fill his belly, but the freezing man as well.

Those thoughts never entered his brain. He stood, his long, pink tongue lolling to one side of his open, panting mouth.

Watching.

Watching and waiting.

From inside the cave, Mint heard the growls plainly, even above the rattling noises of the wind.

The tomahawk, still gripped tight enough to turn her knuckles white, was ready.

Behind her, the small fire crackled as a twig ignited. To Mint, the sound seemed to echo round the small enclosure, making her jump involuntarily, almost letting the tomahawk clatter to the stone floor.

Her breathing steadied down some and she regained composure and she, too, waited.

Her eyes were fixed on the frozen wall of white

that covered the cave entrance. Ice had formed where the heat from the fire had melted the hard-packed snow some, before re-freezing. It seemed, to Mint, to look exactly like a window she'd seen once as a child.

The tribe had been crossing the plains further east, a journey they'd made since time began, following the buffalo. In the distance, a wisp of smoke spiralled into the air and the chief despatched three or four warriors to see what was out there.

The scouting party returned, their tomahawks bloody and a scalp tied to each of their knife belts.

They whooped, parading the bloodied trophies above their heads.

Mint, not older than seven winters, followed the women out to the place where the smoke still rose.

At the foot of an outcrop stood a small, wooden shack, the door wide open and swinging gently in the late autumn breeze.

Already, buzzards were circling high overhead, the smell of death filling the air.

The men took the horses and the rifles; the women took boots and clothing and food. Mint was sent inside to get pots and pans and anything else they could find a use for.

Inside, at the rear of the small shack, Mint saw her first glass window. In it, as clear as daylight, was her own face.

She screamed – but silently for fear of losing face – and ran from the shack, quickly in case anyone saw the panic in her eyes. She stood for a few moments, then turned and went back inside.

The window was still there, and she could see herself mirrored in it, framed by the open door.

She cursed herself for being so foolish. Walking straight up to the window, she touched it tentatively with one finger, expecting it to give, like the still waters of a pond or river.

But it was hard and unforgiving. Her bemused face stared back at her.

She wanted to take this window with her, but before she had time to ask if she could, was bundled out of the way by the rest of the women who had scavenged around the small shack, taking everything that could be carried.

Outside once more, Mint stared through the front door at the glass windowpane as the braves set the shack ablaze.

Her last vision of the glass was as it cracked and then seemed to explode as the hungry flames lapped up the dry lumber.

She hadn't thought about that day until now, as she sat on her haunches, staring at the ice, tomahawk gripped tightly, very tightly.

*

The young wolf ceased struggling. Its lungs were fit to bursting and its body hung limply in the jaws of the older animal. Still he kept hold; making sure and never taking his eyes off the other dog.

When he was certain that the young wolf was dead, he let the body drop to the ground. Then he howled. He howled rather like those braves did, showing off their trophies.

An animal instinct told the older dog that the danger was over. He knew the other wolf wouldn't attack now. He could see its slavering mouth, its tongue dripping saliva as the fresh kill filled its nostrils.

Eat or be eaten, kill or be killed. That was the Law of the Wild.

Turning his back on the drooling animal, the old dog began digging once more. He ignored both the man and the younger wolf; he knew what he must do, but for the life of him, he just plain didn't know why.

FIFTEEN

Although only mid-afternoon, the thick, black clouds that scudded high over the mountain tops made it seem as if the day were about to end.

Henry, vaguely conscious now and then, before drifting off into that sleep that his mind told him meant death, opened one freezing eyelid.

What he saw neither filled him with fear nor dread or disgust. A wolf eating the still-warm remains of another animal right in front of his face.

If he could have done, Henry would have shrugged. Nothing more. His eyelid closed, and he drifted off again.

Henry didn't see the other animal, the one that was frantically digging away at the hard-packed snow, sending a fine spray into the air to be whipped away by the wind. Even if he had, he would probably have shrugged at that, too.

Fine flakes of snow began to fall, almost hail. Slowly, the flakes got bigger and the wind began to deposit them up against tree-trunks and rocks – and Henry.

In less than five minutes, the fine snow-fall turned into another killer-blizzard, obliterating everything. There was no differentiation between sky and land anymore.

It was a whiteout!

The wind, armed now with heavy snow, made a sound that could wake the dead. The roar of the wind and was now accompanied by a pinging sound as ice, mixed with the snow, bounced off every surface.

The dog, seemingly oblivious to the worsening conditions, carried on digging; its front paws scooping out snow to send it shooting backwards between his rear legs.

It was as if the animal knew that every second counted.

A knot of burning wood exploded gently in the campfire, the short, sharp crack echoed slightly in the small cave, enough to make Mint nearly jump out of her skin.

She scolded herself silently, almost dropping the

tomahawk in her near-panic.

She could hear the wind howling outside, it seemed sharper now, and above the sound of the wind, the scratching, incessant and urgent.

Whatever was out there would be through soon.

For the first time, Mint thought of her pony. They'd been able to ride into the valley, but not out. The snow had been sudden and deep and both Mint's pony, her grandfather's pony, and Henry's mule had been set free to forage for themselves.

Mint regretted that decision, but had little choice in the matter. As things turned out, if she'd tethered the animals outside the cave, they'd be dead by now; cold and the avalanche would have taken care of them.

At least now, being free, they had a chance, even if it were only a slim one.

Mint shivered. It wasn't the cold; it was the edge of fear creeping through her bones. The fear of the unknown. She'd already reasoned that if it was Henry digging his way in, he would have called her name by now, given her some sign that all was well.

But the only sounds Mint could hear were the raging wind and the scraping.

Using the last of the bigger branches, Mint thrust it half-way into the campfire. If it was a bear or wolf outside, sniffing out her scent as its next meal, she would use the flaming branch as another weapon. The tomahawk, she knew, would only be a last resort.

Silently, she began chanting, invoking the spirits of her gods to help her; give her the strength and the courage to defeat whatever fate had in store for her.

Another sound filled the cave. A sound that Mint recognized instantly, and it sent a fresh wave of terror down her spine.

A dry, rasping rattle.

Slowly, Mint turned away from the ice-window that she'd been staring at, watching and waiting for whatever appeared. Without moving her body, she scanned the floor of the cave, looking for the source of this new fear.

From the rear of the cave, in a hole blacker than hell where the firelight couldn't reach, she saw two yellow eyes staring blankly, coldly, at her. She couldn't see the forked tongue slipping in and out between those deadly fangs, but she knew it was.

She also knew that the knotty wood that had exploded in the fire had disturbed the hibernating, and the rattle told her what sort of snake it was.

There was nowhere to hide now, nowhere to run; if the attacked her, she would have to be quicker.

Calmly, moving slowly, Mint reached for the

burning branch. Her one salvation was the fact that between her and the rattler, sat the campfire, and she intended to keep it that way.

As she stared at those two devil-eyes, the head of the snake emerged from its lair. The firelight showed that pink tongue flicking incessantly; it reflected off the two large, venom-filled fangs.

The scraping from outside momentarily distracted her and Mint, despite her predicament, allowed herself a wry grin. On one side the snake, behind her, what? A bear? A wolf? Henry?

Shifting slightly so that the cave entrance was now to her right, and the campfire and snake to her left, Mint strained to keep her eyes on both sides at once. She quickly discovered that was impossible, as her eyes darted from one side to the other.

The campfire was keeping the rattlesnake at bay, but Mint knew that once the snake felt threatened, it would take a lot to halt it.

Besides, there was very little wood left, and the fire wouldn't burn forever.

The snake raised its head and in the glow of the fire she saw in those cold, dark eyes, no emotion, no vengeance or revenge, just self-preservation. She knew that the rattler would strike and then return to its lair and hibernation without a second thought.

Holding the now-heavy tomahawk in her left hand, Mint thrust the burning branch towards the snake, it recoiled, but only slightly, and now, adding to the sounds she could hear – the scraping outside, the howling wind, the dead rattle – she heard the snake hiss.

It was a gentle sound in comparison to the other noises, but it was a sound that filled her with dread.

Still on her haunches, she watched as the snake uncoiled and began to slither towards her.

As if guided by a sixth-sense, Henry opened one eye again. Snow and ice was stinging his face, but he didn't notice. The hungry wolf was still attacking and eating the other animal and Henry's ears felt, rather than heard the low-pitched growls of the feeding dog.

With a great deal of effort matched only by his will power and need to survive, Henry found an inner strength.

Slowly bringing up his good arm, Henry prised his face away from the icy tomb he was rapidly being buried in.

Turning his head painfully, he saw the dog. The brightness that had affected his vision, had worn off and, although blurred, he could see the animal frantically digging through the hard-packed snow.

154

Henry tried to raise his upper body, but he'd lost too much energy and strength in merely surviving this long. He lowered his head, breathing in through frozen lips and ice-encrusted nostrils, building his strength and determination.

Then, the digging animal disappeared. One second it was there, the next it had just vanished!

In its place Henry saw a small opening and fear gripped his belly. Not for himself, sudden realization hit him square between the eyes; it was the cave Mint was sheltering in.

The landscape, mostly hidden now by the wild snow flurries, was alien to Henry. There were no markers, nothing to identify the place at all as the same one he'd left only the day before; the avalanche had seen to that.

Mustering up hidden strength, Henry thrust out his good arm and pulled his numb body towards the opening. Inch by inch he neared and, as he did, could feel the warmth coming from the small hole in the snow.

Then a light appeared, faint and flickering, but a light nonetheless.

The glow stung his weak and watery eyes, and Henry began to think he'd gained salvation.

Then he heard the terrifying growls and a high-pitched scream coming from inside the cave.

He opened his mouth to call out, but no sound came. His mind was racing, but his mouth was voiceless. Filled now with a dread worse than he'd ever known, Henry pulled himself closer to the opening, knowing that there wasn't a damn thing he could do, even if he got inside.

SIXTEEN

Henry's eyes flickered open and at once he knew he'd died and gone to heaven.

With tear-filled eyes, Mint stared down at the man she thought she'd never see again, and smiled. She smiled the sweetest smile Henry had ever seen.

'Mint!' Henry choked. His voice didn't seem to belong to him; it was as if someone else was calling out her name.

She smiled once more and stroked his face tenderly.

Henry turned his head towards to dying campfire and there, sitting like a lap-dog, was a wolf.

He tried to sit up and protect Mint, but she held him firmly; seeing the panic in his eyes, she smiled and shook her head. Then she pointed to the side

157

of the wolf and Henry saw the half-chewed rattlesnake.

Mint smiled down into his face and her lips caressed his cheek. Henry forgot the pain in his fingers and toes; the meagre heat coming from the campfire was thawing him out. It took him a while to discover that he was completely naked and wrapped in buffalo- and deer-hide.

Mint, with Henry's head still resting on her lap, was gently massaging his arms and fingers and Henry could feel the pain of the blood beginning to surge once more through his veins.

Mint stopped massaging and brought a tin cup to Henry's lips and poured the warm liquid down his throat. Henry felt the course of the liquid as it eased its way over his tongue, down his throat and he felt it nestle in the empty pit of his stomach.

They were both alive. They would survive.

In the days and weeks and months that followed, Henry was able to piece together the events after he'd left Mint to find a way out of the valley.

They still could only communicate by gesture and smile, but Henry knew that the wolf was the same wolf that had been stalking him all those months back; the scarred and matted fur of the animal's shoulder where Henry had caught him, proved that beyond doubt.

The wolf had saved Henry's life, and Mint's. Attacking the rattlesnake as it leapt through the ice-window, Mint had raised her tomahawk to protect herself, keeping the burning branch aimed at the snake.

The wolf had leapt over her head and, oblivious its own safety, snatched up the surprised snake and literally shook it to death. When the animal was sure it was dead, then, and only then, did he take a bite of it to help stave off his own hunger.

By sign language and with Mint drawing Henry pictures, he learned that the great rumble he'd heard had, indeed, been an avalanche and that Mint had been trapped.

Why the wolf had helped, Henry would never figure out. The fact of the matter was that it did.

The swelling in Henry's arm began to go and he was able to move both arm and fingers, the strength returning as the pain departed.

The worst of the winter snows were behind them, and Henry, after several more weeks of being waited on hand and foot by an eager Mint, ventured outside for the first time.

The air, fresh and clean and cold assailed his senses. The sky, a clear blue made bluer by the snow, surrounded a bright, yellow sun that everyday grew stronger, just as Henry himself did.

They had survived, and Henry knew now that, whatever Mother Nature threw at them in the future – and he and Mint did have a future – the three of them would cope.

Mint, standing behind Henry, smiled. It was a secret smile and, when Henry turned, she took both his hands in hers and placed them on her slightly swollen stomach.

The smile turned into a broad grin, and it was all the message Henry needed.

He pulled her to him and they kissed as he held her tightly in his arms. The wolf, feeling left out, nuzzled both of them, then yawned loudly, sneezed and shook its head, almost losing its balance.

Mint and Henry, still embracing, laughed as they looked at the wolf who had a quizzical look on its face as only dogs can.

Henry knew then that the four of them would survive.